"Trying to

She turned to look at him. "No.

The simple answer alleviated some of the tension knotted in Zac's shoulders. Randi looked like just another bar customer, though normally such a beautiful woman wouldn't be sitting alone.

"So you're not staking me out?"

"I didn't say that."

"So you are?"

"I didn't say that, either." She raised her eyebrows, and the barest hint of a suppressed smile curved her lips.

Very nice, intensely kissable lips.

Snap out of it, Parker. You destroyed that path a long time ago.

Dear Reader,

I'm thrilled to be making my Harlequin Books debut with *A Firefighter in the Family*. It has so many things I love woven together within its pages—a gorgeous and honorable hero, a strong heroine, a devoted dog and the incredibly beautiful shore of the Gulf of Mexico. I also like to throw a dash of mystery into my stories, and you'll see that in the pages that follow.

Miranda "Randi" Cooke followed in the footsteps of her grandfather, father and brothers when she became a firefighter. But a tragic mistake led to estrangement from her family, the end of a romantic relationship that was just beginning, and her leaving her hometown behind. Now she's back—in her professional capacity as a state arson investigator. And in addition to chasing down leads, she also has to face her family and Zac Parker, the man she once loved.

Who can resist a story in which a former love is rekindled? In which the hero and heroine have to work hard to trust each other again and find their happily ever after? Certainly not me.

I hope you enjoy Randi and Zac's story. I'd love to hear what you think. You can e-mail me through my Web site at www.trishmilburn.com.

Happy reading!

Trish Milburn

A Firefighter in the Family

TRISH MILBURN

HARLEQUIN®

TORONTO • NEW YORK • LONDON
AMSTERDAM • PARIS • SYDNEY • HAMBURG
STOCKHOLM • ATHENS • TOKYO • MILAN • MADRID
PRAGUE • WARSAW • BUDAPEST • AUCKLAND

If you purchased this book without a cover you should be aware
that this book is stolen property. It was reported as "unsold and
destroyed" to the publisher, and neither the author nor the
publisher has received any payment for this "stripped book."

ISBN-13: 978-0-373-75232-4
ISBN-10:   0-373-75232-6

A FIREFIGHTER IN THE FAMILY

Copyright © 2008 by Trish Milburn.

All rights reserved. Except for use in any review, the reproduction or
utilization of this work in whole or in part in any form by any electronic,
mechanical or other means, now known or hereafter invented, including
xerography, photocopying and recording, or in any information storage
or retrieval system, is forbidden without the written permission of the
publisher, Harlequin Enterprises Limited, 225 Duncan Mill Road,
Don Mills, Ontario M3B 3K9, Canada.

This is a work of fiction. Names, characters, places and incidents are
either the product of the author's imagination or are used fictitiously,
and any resemblance to actual persons, living or dead, business
establishments, events or locales is entirely coincidental.

This edition published by arrangement with Harlequin Books S.A.

® and TM are trademarks of the publisher. Trademarks indicated with
® are registered in the United States Patent and Trademark Office, the
Canadian Trade Marks Office and in other countries.

www.eHarlequin.com

Printed in U.S.A.

ABOUT THE AUTHOR

Trish Milburn wrote her first book in the fifth grade and has the cardboard-and-fabric-bound, handwritten and colored-pencil-illustrated copy to prove it. That "book" was called *Land of the Misty Gems,* and not surprisingly it was a romance. She's always loved stories with happy endings, whether those stories come in the form of books, movies, TV programs or marriage to her own hero.

A former newspaper and magazine journalist, she took the leap into freelancing so she'd have more time to devote to writing fiction and chasing her dream of being a published novelist. While working toward her first sale, she was an eight-time finalist in the prestigious Golden Heart contest sponsored by Romance Writers of America, winning twice. Other than reading, Trish enjoys traveling (by car or train—she's a terra firma girl!), hiking, nature photography and visiting national parks.

You can visit Trish online at www.trishmilburn.com. Readers also can write to her at P.O. Box 140875, Nashville, TN 37214-0875.

What makes a man a real-life hero? When he tells you every day that he loves you, believes in you even when you don't believe in yourself, and gives his unfailing support even when you want to quit your job to pursue your dream. Shane, I love you bunches. I've dreamed for years of being able to dedicate my first book to you.

My gratitude also goes to the incredible ladies who have been my critique partners throughout the years—Beth Pattillo, Annie Solomon, GayNelle Doll, Michelle Butler and Martha Edinger. I know I wasn't in love with all those red marks on my manuscript pages at the time, but they helped get me to this point.

And to Mary Fechter—thanks for the fast reads, the daily e-mails, the squees over the latest episodes of *Supernatural,* and convincing me to get a TiVo.

Finally, huge thanks to my fabulous agent, Michelle Grajkowski, for being my champion all these years, and to my wonderful editor, Johanna Raisanen, and Kathleen Scheibling for helping my long-held dream come true.

Chapter One

The familiar scent of wet ash invaded Randi's nostrils. Even though the flames had been extinguished and no visible smoke drifted into the bright blue sky, the acrid smell clung to the air, refusing to relinquish its grip. Her stomach twisted. It wasn't the first time fire had blazed in her hometown, but thankfully no one was hurt this time.

From the spot on Sea Oat Road where she now stood, she'd once only been able to see blue-green waves, sugar-white sand and a line of beach homes painted cotton-candy pink, daffodil-yellow and robin's-egg blue. Now she stared at the charred remains of a high-rise condo complex, the soot, crumbling timbers and twisted metal more out of place here in this idyllic spot than at any fire scene she'd ever been sent to investigate.

She glanced toward a side parking lot and spotted a familiar shock of white hair. Smiling, she headed in that direction. When she got within earshot, she called out. "Hey, old man."

Jack Young looked up from where he was stowing equipment in the Number 1 engine. His eyes brightened when he saw her. "Well, I'll be. I haven't seen you in ages." The man she'd always called Uncle Jack came toward her and wrapped her in a bear hug that remained strong for a man closing in on seventy.

"What are you doing still working fires? You should be taking it easy." She phrased her words as teasing, but part of her did worry about him still undertaking the hard labor of firefighting.

"Hon, I've been working so long I don't know how to relax. Besides, this department would fall apart without me." He gestured to a couple of young firefighters at the front of the engine. "These nimwits wouldn't know one end of the hose from the other."

The younger guys snorted.

"So, Steve sent you home to handle this one, huh?" Jack asked as he wiped sweat from his forehead.

Randi ignored the reference to "home." She couldn't think of Horizon Beach like that anymore. It hurt too much. "Yeah. Looks like you had your hands full with this one."

"You can say that again. This baby burned like burning was going out of style. It was amazing to see."

That was saying a lot coming from a guy who'd seen every kind of fire known to man—everything from a lightning-sparked brush fire to a frightening oil-tanker blaze in the Gulf.

She glanced at Jack's profile, saw how he looked into the distance with the familiar expression he got after taking on a big fire. Like he'd stared into the eyes of the beast but lived to tell about it. Jack, more than anyone else she'd ever met, knew fire wasn't just a thing. It was a living, breathing soul bent on destruction. He gave fire the respect it deserved. She just wanted to send it all back to hell.

"So, what's the story?" she asked.

Jack scratched his gray stubble. "Better talk to Will. He was first on the scene. I was bringing up the rear on this one."

"Okay." She'd rather eat sawdust than talk to her brother. "I'll catch you later." Randi walked toward the engine closer to the burned building.

She stepped off the sidewalk where several current Horizon Beach residents and visitors stood speculating about the midnight blaze that had consumed the building.

"Come on, Thor." Her giant black Labrador retriever—one part fire dog, one part best friend—fell into step beside her as she headed for the burned-out shell of the once nearly completed Horizon Vista Resort.

A young fireman stepped out from where he'd been talking to a man in street clothes. "Ma'am, you can't come in here."

She slipped her ID from her pocket. "I'm Randi Cooke with the state fire marshal's office."

He examined the identification card. "You must be—"

"Yeah. Sister to half your department." And daughter of the former chief, and granddaughter to the chief before that.

"Eric and Will are still here." He pointed toward a fire engine, and she saw Will retrieving a tangle of hoses.

She inhaled deeply, but instead of fortifying her for a meeting with her oldest brother, it only filled her nostrils with the scent of ashes. She exhaled through her nose, trying to banish the heavy, choking smell. "Thank you."

Randi headed for the engine. Her nerves jangled, and the muscles in her shoulders tightened despite her internal monologue to stay calm and professional, as she always was at a fire scene. Will looked her way.

Though he should have been expecting her, the widening of his eyes indicated he was surprised to see her.

He'd shucked most of his turnout gear, but the boots, flame-retardant bunker pants and suspenders remained. His blond hair poked out in half a dozen directions from sweat and his helmet.

"Hey, Will."

"Randi. When did you get here?"

She tried to ignore the coolness in his voice, but knowing the reason behind it made that task impossible. "A few minutes ago. Looks like you had a busy night."

"Yeah. Had to call in help from Fort Walton. Place was fully engulfed when we arrived. Went up like it was made of paper." His words came out mechanically, as if he were writing a report—or talking to a stranger.

"Any clue what happened?"

"No. Wouldn't be surprised if it's arson."

"What makes you say that?"

He pointed toward the rubble. "The only people happy about this place were the tourism bureau, the tax assessor and the builder."

"Jack didn't mention arson."

Will glanced toward the older man. "Hell, the old coot probably slept through half the fire. He wasn't on duty, so the guys from Fort Walton got here before he did."

"He should retire."

Will sighed. Obviously this topic had been broached many times. "Too stubborn, even though he's not as fast or strong as he used to be."

She hoped Jack would change his mind about retirement before he or someone else got hurt. But that thought brought back memories she'd rather not explore.

"So, who's the owner?"

He exhaled. "Guy named Bud Oldham from Tampa." Will frowned, and his fair complexion grew pinker than when he'd spotted her.

They'd already spoken more this morning than they had in the past two years combined. Of course, not all of that was Will's fault. Still, her job required digging for information. "Oldham around during the fire?"

"Hell, I don't know." He pitched his gloves into the truck. "I was too busy to canvass the crowd." He stalked alongside the engine and slammed two equipment doors.

Randi's jaw clenched, but she forced her muscles to relax. Forced herself to remember that she'd driven this wedge herself and she had to live with it. "I'm just doing my job, Will."

She tugged gently on Thor's leash, needing to immerse herself in work so she'd forget why the oldest of the Cooke siblings would never forgive her. Why being the baby of the family and a girl had sent her fleeing from her once-loving home. How one mistake could change so many lives.

As she sloshed through the mucky sand caused by the rush of water from the hoses the night before, she spotted Eric headed toward her. Soot darkened his pale skin, and he sported a hairstyle like his older brother's. She remembered that sweaty, itchy feeling and resisted the urge to scratch her scalp. In contrast to Will, the youngest of her four older brothers smiled at her.

"Hey, sis. I wondered if they'd send you to work this one." Eric reached down and rubbed Thor's head between his ears, earning a yip of greeting in response.

"Yeah, Steve's daughter is getting married today."

Her boss had been in a tizzy all week, alternating between telling everyone how beautiful a bride his daughter was going to be and cursing how much the wedding was costing him.

"And you're missing it?"

"I'm never glad for a fire, but I can't say I'm heart-broken to miss La Prima Donna's nuptials."

Eric laughed, but his expression changed when he glanced over her shoulder. "Will looks like he's ready to bite the head off an alligator."

"Yeah, well, some things never change." She tried to keep the bitterness out of her voice but wasn't successful.

"You two at it already?"

"No, I walked away."

"It's been nearly three years. Are you guys ever going to talk about what happened?"

Randi sighed. "I tried. Besides, he's right." As much as it made her heart ache to admit it.

"It was an accident. It wasn't—"

She stopped Eric with a quick, cutting hand gesture. "Let's focus on figuring out what happened here. Any ideas?"

Randi retreated into her job, quizzing her brother about the fire and the building's owner.

"Eric, come on, we got work to do." Will's voice wasn't that of an older brother, but rather a superior officer.

"Coming." Eric looked back at her. "You'll be around?"

"Yeah." She scanned the rubble. "Looks like this might take a while."

"You staying at Mom and Dad's?" He always asked the question, even though the answer never changed.

"No. I'll get a room." She ignored the sad look in Eric's blue eyes.

"I'll call you on your cell then. We'll grab a bite."

"Eric!" Will sounded more irritated.

"Go on before he really gets his drawers in a wad." She smiled, trying to make light of the situation.

Taking a chance at angering their older brother, Eric leaned over and kissed her on the cheek. "I'd hug you but I'm pretty rank at the moment."

"Thanks for keeping your sweat to yourself."

He smiled again, his white teeth standing out against his blackened face. "Catch ya later." He slogged through the mud in his splattered boots, and she remembered when they'd been kids, running through puddles after a fast-moving coastal rain.

"Let's get to it," she said to Thor as she stirred the ash. He began sniffing the remains of the building, searching for accelerant.

When the breeze shifted and replaced the scent of char with the freshness of the ocean, Randi breathed deeply and closed her eyes, remembering how she used to crawl up onto her parents' roof to soak in the sun and watch the waves roll in. When she wrapped this case, she'd take some vacation time to relax. Every firebug in Florida had picked this spring to torch all available combustibles, and the worst drought in a decade wasn't helping. She and Thor were more in demand than ever.

"You going to catch the bastard who did this?"

At the edge of the burned-out area stood a tall man with gray hair and a tan that would rival George Hamilton's. This guy must spend every daylight hour outside without a drop of sunscreen.

Randi raised from her crouched position. "Mr. Oldham?"

"Yeah."

Randy carefully picked her way across the building's innards toward its owner. "Any idea what might have started this fire?"

"I have no doubt someone torched the place," he said.

Randi crossed her arms and watched Oldham for the slightest change of expression. She kept her voice even and nonaccusatory as she asked, "What makes you say that?"

"Locals have an aversion to progress."

"So there was opposition to the construction?" She'd once known every piece of gossip in town, but not much Horizon Beach news made it to her present home in Pensacola.

"You could say that."

"From whom?"

He gestured inland. "Damn neighbors, a park ranger, some of those freak greenies. Hell, might even be that stupid bar guy," Oldham said. "Don't think I'm his favorite person, either."

She asked about each potential suspect and took thorough notes on them.

"You mentioned a 'bar guy.' Can you be more specific?"

"Parker. Owns a little shack of a bar on the beach."

Her heart beat wildly for a moment at the mention of the name Parker, until her mind caught up and struck the possibility of it being Zac Parker. Zac was a firefighter, not a bartender.

Oldham pointed to the southeast. "I tried to buy him out, wanted to put a pool where he's at, but he wouldn't budge."

Randi cloaked herself in her professional persona

instead of memories. "Sounds as though your condos weren't too popular. Why build them here?"

He directed his "watch your smart mouth, girlie" gaze at her, but she didn't look away. She'd interviewed too many people who'd torched their own homes and businesses for the insurance money to let this guy bother her.

"Have you seen the rest of the Florida coast?" he asked. "High-rise condos are a dime a dozen, hard to make them stand out among the hordes. Here, it'd be the only one."

"For now."

"That's what matters." Oldham looked at the heap that used to be his investment. "You really think you can find out how this happened?"

Thor barked, deep and throaty, the distinctive bark that meant he'd completed a mission. She and Oldham looked to where Thor stood at a spot close to what had been the southwest corner of the building.

Randi nodded toward Thor. "That's a step in the right direction."

ZAC PARKER CURSED under his breath when the breeze shifted, bringing the smoky smell of the burned building into his open-air bar. Once, he'd considered that smell a part of everyday life. Now, it just brought back bad memories.

"Guess he ticked off one too many people, huh?"

Zac looked up from where he was pulling a cold Budweiser from the bottle cooler beneath the bar. Adam Canfield, his friend and regular bar patron, stared at the remains of Bud Oldham's controversial venture into Gulf Coast realty.

"Maybe," Zac said. "Could have been wiring or someone forgot to turn off a torch."

Adam looked back at Zac and accepted the beer. "You don't really believe that."

Zac shrugged. "Don't know. Not my problem." He would not admit to any instinctive curiosity about the fire. Or the sliver of satisfaction he'd experienced thinking about that pompous jackass Oldham getting a little payback. He didn't like the feeling. He'd spent nearly a decade of his life fighting fires, first in Tallahassee, then in Horizon Beach, before he'd walked away.

And the Beach Bum, with its thatch roof and position next to the condos, could have been destroyed if the wind had blown the opposite way and carried embers in that direction. Fire had destroyed his life once. He was damn lucky it hadn't performed an encore.

"Well, it's gonna be somebody's. Hell, maybe Oldham got tired of all the opposition and burned it himself."

Wanting to steer the conversation away from Bud Oldham and fires, Zac pointed at the fishing pier jutting into the Gulf of Mexico. "They catching much?"

Adam glanced toward the pier, which was already lined with people and their fishing poles. "Mainly pompano and channel bass," he said as he gave Zac a look that showed he knew he was deliberately changing the subject.

That was Adam—Mr. Observant. He was also the closest Zac had to a best friend. After a dozen years of the army telling him how to dress and sending him to one hot, dusty location after another, Adam had said "screw it" and returned to Florida where the sand actually had some water next to it. He'd plopped down in the Beach Bum after his first day as a Horizon Beach resident and announced, "Sand, surf, fishing, cold beer and bikinis as far as the eye can see. I've died and gone to heaven."

Zac had laughed and given him a beer on the house.

The two of them had a similar take on life—the less stress and responsibility, the better. For Zac, the Beach Bum was a bar where he could listen to the ocean all day and call the shots. For Adam, the fishing pier concession paid the bills and afforded him the opportunity to watch said bikinis all day and fish to his heart's content.

"Now what is wrong with this picture?" Adam asked.

Zac looked up the beach. A woman with a blond ponytail and one heck of a big black Lab walked toward the bar. "You mean that there's a woman on the beach who isn't wearing a bikini or the fact that the dog looks like he might be part horse?"

"There's a dog?"

"Jeez, you're incurable."

"Thor, stay," she said from the edge of the bar.

"Thor, huh?" Adam evidently thought noticing the dog would win him points with its owner. "That seems appropriate."

Zac was about to make a smart-ass comment about Adam's flirting when he realized he recognized her voice. He looked up as she stepped into the bar and shoved her sunglasses onto the top of her head. His hand tightened around the edge of the bar.

Randi Cooke.

She ignored Adam and turned her attention toward Zac. Her forehead scrunched, and he could nearly hear the gears turning behind those gorgeous blue eyes of hers. She had that out-of-place expression on her face—like when you go on vacation and bump into someone from back home.

"Zac?"

"Randi," he said with as little emotion as possible. Not as easy as it sounded.

"You two know each other?" Adam asked from his scoping-the-hotties perch.

"We're acquainted," Zac said. He turned his back and straightened bottles of liquor that didn't need straightening. He ignored the awkward silence behind him. What he wouldn't have given for some warning of her arrival.

"Well, I'm not," Adam said.

"Randi Cooke with the state fire marshal's office," she said, her formal introduction and tone quashing any hope that she'd just happened by for a drink.

A Cooke investigating a fire. Not to mention a Cooke he'd wronged and who had fled town partly because of him. Just what he needed. Time to nip this in the ol' bud and send her on her way.

He turned toward her and leaned back against the metal sink. "Before you ask, I wasn't around when the fire started," he said as he nodded toward what remained of the condos.

She raised her eyebrows.

"Doesn't take a genius to figure out you're here to ask if I saw anything suspicious, not to ask for a martini," he said. "The bar closes at one. The fire started after that."

"The call came in at one-seventeen, to be exact."

Zac stiffened. He scanned the few patrons at the outer edge of the bar. They apparently hadn't heard her. "You'd better not be accusing me of anything." Been down that road with her family, didn't want to revisit.

Surprise widened her eyes for a moment. "I don't recall doing so. Is there a reason I should?" she asked, a coolness seeping into her words.

"Runs in the family," he muttered.

"What?"

"Well, gotta go," Adam said as he grabbed his beer and fled.

Zac barely noticed Adam leaving. Instead, he stared at Randi. Damn her for standing so close while being so distant, as if they'd never met, while he wanted to crush something with his bare hand at the thought that suspicion might touch him again. What irked him even more was that in the midst of the chilly reunion, he couldn't help noticing she was even prettier now than when he'd seen her last. Her bright eyes seemed wiser, her body more toned, her hair even more blond and silky. Every aspect of her physical appearance made it more difficult to deal with her.

He broke eye contact. "Listen, Oldham tried to buy me out. I said no. He was ticked. End of story."

"Just how bad was this disagreement?"

There she was doing it again, acting as if he were a stranger, as if they hadn't once worked side by side. As if they hadn't once been more than co-workers. Still a Cooke through and through—despite everything that had happened.

Zac moved to the edge of the oak bar and leaned down so his voice didn't carry. "Bad enough to think tossing the jackass in the Gulf might be amusing—yes. Bad enough to burn his eyesore to the ground—no. Now you know and can move on to the next person on your list."

"You're a bit belligerent for an innocent man, aren't you?"

Yeah, he was belligerent. It felt like déjà vu all over again. "Anyone would be if unfounded accusations were being cast at him."

She caught and held his gaze, and for a second he thought he glimpsed a sliver of the old Randi. He couldn't help the yearning for what they'd once shared, what might have been, however ill-advised that might be.

"I'm not accusing you, Zac," she said. "I'm just asking questions. Looking for the truth."

Zac's stomach knotted. The last time someone had questioned him about a fire and he'd told the truth, they'd rewarded him with handcuffs and a trip to jail.

He wouldn't be falsely accused again.

Chapter Two

Zac huffed and turned away as he shoved individual wine bottles into a glass-fronted cooler to chill.

"You don't seem to like me very much anymore," Randi said, trying to sound as if she didn't care one way or the other.

"I'm busy. I have a business to run."

"Yeah, about that—what's with the whole bartender shtick?" Not that he didn't look yummier than any cold, fruity drink he could serve up.

Randi leaned one arm against the edge of the bar and stared at Zac's back, a very nice, muscled back from what she remembered, and his tanned forearms. When he glanced to the side, she eyed his profile. Short, dark hair. Strong jawline. Stubborn. Why, of all the people in Horizon Beach, had she crossed paths with Zac Parker? And why did the mere sight of him still make her pulse race as if it were trying to break free of her veins?

A blonde in a pink bikini with a flowered wrap around her hips wandered up to the bar and asked for two beers. Randi waited while Zac turned, pulled the bottles from the cooler and took the girl's money. He didn't ogle the eye candy, and Randi was annoyed by how much that pleased her. Which made no sense, considering the circumstances the last time they'd seen each other.

He looked up, his expression casual. "You're still here?"

"Let's leave past animosity in the past, shall we?" She was here in her professional capacity, and what they'd once meant to each other wasn't relevant to the task at hand.

"Fine." He bit out the word as if it was anything but fine. As if to contradict his tone, he placed a lemonade in front of her. He glanced up, caught her gaze for a moment before breaking eye contact. "I have a good memory."

She didn't let it show, but she was shocked he'd remembered.

Zac leaned against a metal cooler and crossed his arms.

Why was he so hostile? She was the one with that right, not him. "I have to investigate every angle. You know that."

"Dig to my birth certificate if it makes you happy, but don't jump to conclusions before you know what you're talking about," he said.

Those words sliced at her. She didn't rush headlong into things anymore. She'd learned her painful lesson.

"Nice to see you've matured since I saw you last." She couldn't help it. The bitterness just tumbled out. Better to sound bitter than brokenhearted, though.

Four lobster-human hybrids stepped into the bar and eased their sunburned selves into the chairs surrounding a nearby table. A surfer type approached the opposite end of the long bar, and Zac moved away without another word or glance in her direction.

Fine. She knew where to find him.

She noticed his liquor license on the wall. Why on earth was he tending bar instead of fighting fires? Oldham would have her believe Zac had started setting them instead. But no matter how much he'd hurt her, she couldn't picture him as an arsonist.

Zac's deep voice drew her attention. He was even sexier than she remembered—and what she'd remembered had been plenty sexy. Alone in her mind, she could admit she was still attracted to him, even if she couldn't forgive him.

ZAC WATCHED Randi Cooke retrace her steps toward the burned-out condos, her wake sucking him back almost three years.

"Dude, you're about to pop a blood vessel."

Zac redirected his gaze to find Adam had sauntered back to the bar and was tapping his temple. "I'm fine."

"Then I'd hate to see a man on the verge of a stroke."

Zac turned to throw some empty cartons in the trash so he wouldn't bite off Adam's head. His friend had been a beach staple for barely two years, hadn't been there when all hell broke loose in Zac's life.

Adam took a drink of his beer as he watched Randi disappear over the dunes. "What's the story with the babe?"

"No story."

"Right."

"We went out a few times, that's all." He wasn't willing to recount all the details, but he'd give Adam enough to get him off his case.

"So, how bad was your argument with Oldham?" Adam asked.

"If you're going to play cop, you can just go back to the pier."

Adam raised his hands. "Chill. I'm on your side."

Zac braced his palms against the top of the cooler. "Sorry. She just raised my hackles."

Adam nodded but looked like he suspected there was more behind Zac's reaction. "Understandable. Having the ex interrogate you—not exactly what you expected when you got up this morning."

Actually, when he'd arrived at work and seen the devastation next door, he'd imagined such an encounter. But he'd figured on one of Randi's brothers doing the interrogation. He wasn't sure that wouldn't have been better. At least he didn't have any guilt wrapped up in his feelings toward them.

"Anything you want to share in case your Nancy Drew shows up at the pier asking questions?"

Zac shook his head. "There's nothing to know. Oldham wanted to buy me out, I said no, that was the end of it."

Adam stared at him for a moment, as if maybe he didn't believe him. Well, that was Adam's problem, not his. He was damned tired of explaining himself, especially to people who were supposed to be his friends.

RANDI WALKED out of her hotel room's bathroom toweling the excess water from her long hair. After a full day of sniffing rubble and accompanying her while she interviewed witnesses, Thor lay stretched out on one of the beds watching the *Eukanuba Dog Show* on Animal Planet.

"Checking out the babes, huh?"

Thor licked his chops as a female husky strutted her stuff.

"You're so predictable. It's always the blue-eyed girls."

Randi slipped into white cargo pants and an orange tee, thankful to be out of smoky clothes. She propped her pillows behind her against the headboard and pulled out her case notebook.

She scanned through the list of names and didn't scratch any off, not even eighty-year-old Penelope "Busybody" Jones. Randi couldn't imagine the woman who looked like Barbara Bush's twin doddering across Sea Oat Road with a can of gasoline and a box of matches in the middle of the night, but she'd seen stranger things happen.

She leaned back and thought about Zac's reaction to her questioning. Red-flag city. Her eyes drifted closed as she pictured his tight facial expressions, his tense body language. His finely toned body. She swallowed.

Even though his status as a potential suspect gave her the distance she needed from him, she couldn't believe he was really guilty. But he didn't have to know that. The mere thought of someone she'd once cared about, a fellow firefighter, being the culprit sickened her. But he wasn't a firefighter anymore, was he? Why? After all, he'd once sacrificed friendship and the possibility of something more for the job.

Her cell phone rang, and she answered while making notes for the next morning's itinerary.

"How'd it go today?" Steve asked.

Did her boss ever take a day off? "I should be asking you the same question. How's the happy couple?"

"On their way to Cozumel. What have you found out?"

Randy shook her head. If there was one thing that could be said for Steve Preston, it was that he was dedicated to the job. If the entire state of Florida caught fire simultaneously, he'd find a way to have a working knowledge of every single case to which his investigators were assigned.

"Thor's keeping his reputation intact. I sent a sample off to the lab, but it smelled like gasoline."

"Suspects?"

"Well, the consensus is that the builder is a jerk and the condo project unpopular. The suspect list is turning into a cast of thousands."

As soon as she hung up a few minutes later, her cell rang again. "Hello?"

"Hey, sis. Where ya staying?" Eric asked.

"The Coral Inn on Gulf."

"I see the state is putting you up in the fancy places."

"Ha-ha." How good it felt to talk to him. The full impact of how much she missed him and the rest of her family made her suck in a shaky breath.

"Want some dinner?"

"You buying?"

"You're the one with the cushy state job."

Randi rolled her eyes. "Yeah, I'm making so much money I don't know what to do with it all."

"Okay, I'll spring. Pick you up in ten."

Randi slipped on a pair of white canvas mules, an oddity in her collection of dirty boots and athletic shoes. Even her running shoes were scuffed and smelly from her morning jogs.

When Eric pulled into the parking lot, Thor leaped into the bed of the black Dodge Ram without being told. Randi slid into the passenger seat.

"Hey, you clean up decent," Eric said.

Randi sniffed the air. "You, too. I don't smell you quite so much anymore."

Eric punched her lightly in the arm, like he'd done as a kid. It caused a pang in her chest, and she wished things were that simple and carefree again.

"So, where we going?"

Eric didn't answer, but he turned east, away from most of the town's restaurants. Toward home.

Anger and anxiety made her muscles tighten. She stared hard at Eric's profile, but he refused to look her way. "Damn it. You ambushed me."

"Come on," he pleaded. "It's not like I'm dragging you to prison or the gates of hell."

"No, just the land of thinly veiled hostility."

"It's not that bad, and you know it."

"I don't know it. You just refuse to see what's right in front of your nose. Now turn around."

"No."

Randi looked at her brother in stunned surprise.

"Carol will have my hide," Eric said, sheepish.

If there existed someone more determined than Eric to rebuild the burned bridges in the Cooke family, it was her sister-in-law Carol, Will's wife. The irony never failed to strike Randi. If Will was strong and determined and sometimes bullheaded, Carol was every bit his equal but somehow managed to be a sweet person at the same time.

"That's freaking fantastic." Randi crossed her arms and watched the shops of downtown Horizon Beach zip by as Eric drove toward their parents' house on the outskirts of town. She hated having control of a situation taken from her.

"Give it a rest. You're here at Thanksgiving and Christmas. What difference does the day make?"

"I have time to prepare for the holidays."

"So now you have to 'prepare' to see your family?"

"When half that family still holds a grudge against me, yes." Not that there wasn't cause. Still, it hurt.

"Randi, it's time to move on."

She turned toward her brother and pierced him with the stare that put fear into the hearts of otherwise heartless arsonists. "Did you happen to hear Will this morning? Did you notice I wasn't exactly the person he most wanted to see?"

"He was tired. We were up all night."

"Fatigue doesn't put that look in a man's eyes."

Eric didn't argue further, and Randi was sorry. She needed the outlet to vent steam. Honestly, she'd love to reconnect with her family, to experience the intense love and camaraderie they'd once enjoyed. But no longer could she hang out with her brothers and father and talk shop. It hurt that they didn't seem to want to, either, but she couldn't blame them.

When Eric parked in front of their parents' two-story on Sand Dune Drive, Randi let out a long, anxiety-filled breath. The number of vehicles in the driveway and on the side of the street struck her as odd. "Why is everyone here?"

"It's an engagement party. Karl finally asked Shellie."

Despite her roiling emotions, Randi smiled. At least she was home for a happy occasion. Hopefully, everyone would be in a good mood. "It's about time. So, that leaves you as the sole Cooke bachelor, huh?"

He smiled, looking relieved as the tenseness in his body eased. "Unless we count you."

"We don't, seeing as how I don't even have time to date."

"Hon, there's always time to date."

She thought of a romantic dinner on the beach, the

sound of the waves and soft music mingling. Zac Parker appeared in her daydream.

Good grief, she must be rattled if she was fantasizing about the man who'd crushed her heart when she was already hurting. She needed a good, stiff drink and about a month in the Bahamas after this job.

She started to ask Eric about when Zac had left the department and why but decided she didn't even want to utter his name and add to her current discomfort. Plus, she was itching to see Karl so she could offer a good-natured "I told you so." She hoped he'd set aside the past for at least tonight, long enough to accept the sisterly barb.

Thor jumped out of the truck and padded after her.

"Stay," she said when they stepped onto the porch.

He whined then plopped down on the porch and laid his muzzle on his outstretched paws.

"Trust me, boy, I'd rather stay out here with you."

Randi trailed Eric as they passed through the empty living room and followed the sound of loud Cooke voices coming from the back of the house. When they reached the kitchen, their mother looked up from frosting a cake. Inga's eyes widened. She set down the frosting and came over to hug Randi.

"Honey, what a nice surprise."

Randi hated how she dissected her mother's words for any hint of falseness.

Inga pulled away and wiped back a strand of her hair, still its Norwegian white-blond even at age sixty.

Carol stepped into the kitchen from the deck. In a house full of blond, blue-eyed Cookes, the petite brunette stood out.

"I'm so glad you came," Carol said. She didn't

pause before crossing the room to give Randi an enthusiastic hug. Having such a true-blue ally felt good, even when Randi herself didn't believe she deserved it.

Randi wondered if she would have been invited to this gathering had she not already been in town. The pang in her chest caused her to bite down on her bottom lip. She'd gotten on with her life after leaving Horizon Beach, but the passage of nearly three years had done nothing to ease the pain of her loss.

"So, when did Karl pop the big question?" she asked Carol, determined to get through the night without falling apart.

"Yesterday."

"This is one quick party."

"We wanted to cement the deal before Karl had second thoughts." Inga laughed, well aware of her third son's ability to slide out of things as if he were doused in oil.

"Good point."

Carol snaked her arm through Randi's. "Come on outside."

Randi balked. "I think I'll stay in here for a bit."

"Nonsense. Karl and Shellie are out there taking a lot of ribbing. You don't want to miss this."

"I'll—"

"You never win an argument with me, so quit trying." She leaned close to Randi's ear. "Don't worry, I'll protect you."

Randi had to laugh. At five foot two, Carol stood a full seven inches shorter than her and didn't have near the muscle tone. Somehow, chasing a two-year-old around didn't quite build the body the same way five-mile runs and swimming did. Still, Carol Cooke wasn't someone ever bested in an argument.

Despite the tightening in her gut, Randi allowed her sister-in-law to lead her onto the deck filled with the scents of grilling shrimp and steaks and the sounds of her family.

The scene unfolded as if from one of those *Matrix* movies where everyone stops in midmotion. If she were lucky, she'd disappear before they remembered to move. She glanced over and saw her father, a once big and towering man, sitting in his wheelchair.

The wheelchair she'd put him in.

Chapter Three

"Add some shrimp to the grill," Carol said. "We've got one more person who wanted to give Karl the teasing he deserves."

Will, who was tending the meat on the grill, stared at them for a moment before turning his back and adding more shrimp.

The awkwardness eased gradually as conversations resumed, like the slow receding of a wave back out to sea. Randi wished she could ride that wave into open water, where the expanse of blue gently rolled and soothed.

Shellie crossed the deck and gave Randi a hug. She returned the gesture, grateful for another friendly face. If it weren't for Eric and the women in this family, she'd be a total outcast.

"Randi, how have you been?" Her father sounded like he genuinely wanted to know, but the deep warmth and vitality his voice used to hold was absent.

"Fine, thanks. You?"

Everyone seemed to hold their breath as they awaited his answer, as if he might suddenly yell, *I'm a paraplegic, how the hell do you think I feel?* Instead, he said simply, "Okay."

Randi had to alleviate the tension or she was going to snap. She looked at Karl. "So, you popped the question. I remember saying I would relish this day so I could say, 'I told you so.'"

Karl offered a half grin. "You're not the only one."

He sounded so forlorn that everyone, including his new wife-to-be, laughed.

The laughter broke the tension for a few moments, but when they sat down to eat, it returned. Randi stood to the side, not sure where to sit. She imagined that if she took a seat the brother next to her would move.

Considering they'd not done so during previous family gatherings, she didn't know why she thought they suddenly would. Maybe it was the fact that a fire and not a holiday had brought her to Horizon Beach this time. A fire that would remind them all of that horrible day when their lives had changed.

But she needn't have worried. Inga guided her to a chair between her and Carol. A safe zone where she had at least the sliver of hope that she'd be able to eat something.

Though conversations gradually picked up around her, the one topic avoided was her reason for being in town. Her brothers and father had likely picked the fire apart molecule by molecule, but none of that discussion materialized now. Not even Eric brought it up, though she caught him watching her a couple of times with an expression that said he wished he could make it all normal again.

Her mother reached over at one point and patted her hand, a loving gesture but one that fell short of demanding her other offspring welcome their sister with wide-open arms. Maybe Inga loved her while still holding her responsible for her father's condition. Could the two feelings coexist?

Randi tried to take another bite of shrimp, but it seemed to expand in her mouth with each chew. When she attempted to swallow, it nearly choked her.

She looked over at her father, who was talking baseball with Josh, the second oldest and quietest of her brothers. The Great Avoider, they'd always called him, because he didn't like conflict. He'd never said anything negative toward her regarding the fire that had ended their father's career, but he hadn't stood up for her, either.

They sat outside, so close to the ocean she could hear the tide coming in, but Randi couldn't draw in a deep breath. How odd to feel she needed fresh air when she was in the midst of it. She stood and picked up her plate.

"Thanks for dinner. It was delicious." She looked at Karl and Shellie. "Congratulations on the engagement."

"Don't leave so soon," Carol said. "The party's just getting started."

"Sorry. I've got a ton of work to do." Randi's heart cried out for her father to ask her to stay, but he said nothing.

Before anyone could say anything, she hurried to the kitchen, deposited her food and paper plate in the trash. The door opened behind her, but she didn't turn as she dumped the ice in her cup down the sink.

"I wish you'd stay," Inga said, sorrow thickening in her voice.

Randi closed her eyes and took a deep breath. "I'm sorry to rush, but I have lots of notes to go over and people to call before the trail goes cold." She pasted a smile on her face as she turned to face her mother. "Thanks again for dinner."

The sadness from Inga's voice crept into her eyes, her mother's heart knowing work wasn't the reason Randi was departing so quickly. Inga sighed then went to the refrigerator and pulled out a large plate. "I know how much you love my cheesecake, so I want you to take a slice with you."

"You don't have to do that."

"I insist. I have plenty."

Randi watched as her mother placed the generous slab of cheesecake on a plastic saucer with a plastic fork and covered it with cling wrap. She filled a small disposable foam cup with strawberry topping. Randi's mouth watered at the remembered rich, creamy texture of the dessert.

Inga handed the cup and saucer to Randi and kissed her cheek. "Call me before you go home. Maybe we can have lunch."

Randi fought tears and nodded. "Okay." She headed for the front door before she lost her composure. She hadn't been this shaken in a long time. She was halfway to the street, Thor on her heels, when Eric caught up with her.

"Go on back and enjoy yourself," she said.

"I'll take you to your hotel first." He sounded sad and sorry he'd forced the situation on her.

She stopped walking but didn't look at him. She didn't want him to see the tears threatening. "I'll walk. It's a nice evening."

"You're sure?"

"Yeah." Without making eye contact, she lifted onto her toes to give his cheek a quick peck. "Thanks for trying." She headed for the sidewalk that led back to Sea Oat Road.

She'd gone half a mile when she reached the first public beach access. She took the boardwalk over the dunes and headed for the compacted part of the shoreline where the edge of the waves wet the sand. She kicked off her mules and carried them in one hand as she let the feel of the sand beneath her toes comfort her.

She focused on the sound of the surf and the fresh feel of the breeze and imagined them both carrying her worries away. She remembered that from one of the dozens of self-help books she'd read when the nightmares and bouts of crying after the accident had finally worn her down to where she could barely function.

A therapist was probably what she'd needed, but Miranda Leann Cooke had enough of her father and older brothers in her to avoid a shrink and convince herself she could handle it on her own. For the most part, she'd done okay. For now, that would have to suffice.

As the sun dipped below the horizon and the first dim stars twinkled, Randi wondered if her walk on the beach had been the right choice. Couples soaking in the romance of the scene lined the shore, nuzzling on blankets or walking hand in hand. Other than a couple of joggers, she was the only solo stroller.

Not only could she not find comfort in family, the latest man in her life had decided that her job kept her away too much and had moved on to someone else. Pete hadn't been her great love, but the loneliness still got to her during weak moments. And reinforced the fact that if she cared about someone, they always let her down.

Twenty-nine and unattached. It wasn't as if her biological clock was ticking—she wasn't even sure she had one. Still, it would be nice to have someone to share life's ups and downs with, someone with whom to stroll on the beach, go on a dolphin-sightseeing cruise, someone to jog with in the mornings. Someone who wouldn't abandon her.

Again, Zac's face popped into her mind, only adding to her foul mood. Romance with Zac Parker was a long-gone possibility.

She stopped and watched a pelican glide through the air before nosediving into the water. Thor nuzzled her hand and looked up at her. "Not that you're not a wonderful companion," she said to him. "It's just not the same."

Randi sat down and let the edge of the cool water tickle her toes each time the waves rolled in. She thought of her brothers. Will, married and the father of a two-year-old son. Josh, married. Karl, engaged. When Eric finally paired up, she'd be the only one left alone. Why did she suddenly feel as if a dark, hungry chasm was growing inside her heart?

Normally she stayed too busy to be lonely, but being back here, seeing her family—not to mention Zac—brought that buried loneliness to the surface where it stung and ached.

The breeze brought the sound of giggles. She turned to see a young couple kissing and laughing a few yards up the beach.

She wondered what that would be like—to be that carefree, that happy, that in love. She'd been that girl once, before she'd dared to follow in her brothers' footsteps, before she'd gone into that fire, before Zac Parker had sided with the Cooke men against her despite how close they had grown. She'd been that girl once, but no more.

A WARM SUMMER Saturday night, and the joint was hopping. Just the way Zac liked it, especially after the day he'd had. Keeping busy was key to not focusing on his latest encounter with someone looking to make him an arson suspect—or the fact that person was Randi. What the hell was it with his karma?

He handed three beers to a customer and turned to the next only to find Randi Cooke standing there. His jaw muscles tensed.

She held up a hand. "I just want a bottle of water. And do you have an empty bowl?"

"An empty bowl?"

"So I can give Thor half the water."

Zac looked across the packed bar but didn't see the dog.

"Don't worry. He's on the beach."

Zac fished a bottle of water out of the cooler and handed it to her along with one of the disposable peanut bowls.

In return, she handed him three dollars, said thanks and walked toward the front corner of the bar. He watched as she poured part of the water into the bowl then stepped down into the sand and walked a short distance. She bent out of sight before standing back where he could see her.

After the way he'd wronged her, the only reason she could be here was the investigation. It certainly wasn't to reconnect, no matter how much he'd once wanted that.

"Hey, can I get a cosmo?" A girl wearing a tiny, lime-green bikini top stood at the bar.

An influx of new customers and those seeking seconds…and thirds…kept him busy, but his eyes continued wandering back to where Randi had taken a seat and appeared to be eating. The Beach Bum's menu included only beverages and peanuts, so she'd brought it with her. Sometimes she caught him looking, other times she was either eyeing the crowd or staring toward the whitecaps of the waves against the much darker expanse of water. What was she up to?

Fifteen minutes passed, then thirty. Finally, he broke. "Be back in a minute," he said to Suz, the other bartender. He wove his way through the laughter, but it didn't penetrate his sour mood. What rolled inside him was more like a potent mixture of anger, frustration and a dash of the desire to flee. She had yet to accuse him of anything, but he couldn't banish the feeling that it was only a matter of time. She was, after all, a Cooke. And she'd probably relish some payback against him.

Not for the first time, he wondered if he should've left Horizon Beach after he'd been cleared of the arson charges two years before. But he liked the little town and didn't want to look like a coward. And he'd savored the idea of the Cookes having to see him and live with their mistakes. Petty, yes, but he wasn't any more perfect than the next guy.

When he drew closer to Randi, he noticed how much prettier she was in her casual clothes. And when she wasn't questioning him. Her ponytail hung down her back, looking so silky he wanted to touch it. Man, he had no right to make fun of Adam's hormones with the way his reacted to Randi—despite their past and the reason she was back in Horizon Beach. She appeared oblivious to the reveling going on around her. Rather, she stared toward the Gulf, her forehead creased.

"Trying to figure out how to bust me?"

She turned her head to look at him. A moment passed before her look of concentration faded. "No."

The simple answer, combined with her more casual attire and the appearance that her thoughts had been elsewhere, alleviated some of the tension knotted in his shoulders. She looked like just another bar customer, though normally such a beautiful woman wouldn't be sitting alone.

"You're not staking me out?"

"I didn't say that."

"So you are?"

"I didn't say that either." She raised her eyebrows, and the barest hint of a suppressed smile curved her lips.

Very nice, intensely kissable lips.

Snap out of it, Parker. You destroyed that path a long time ago.

"I don't want you harassing my customers."

"Have you seen me talking to any of them?" The semismile was gone, as if she'd remembered who he was and what he'd done to her.

He stared at her, trying to figure her out.

She pointed at the chair opposite her. "Have a seat."

"I'm working."

"And yet you had enough time to come over to talk to me."

She didn't miss a beat, damn it. He looked back toward the front of the bar. Suz did seem to have the flow of business under control. Maybe he could do some questioning of his own. He pulled out the chair and sank into it.

Randi scanned the crowd. "Looks like you've got a good business here."

He examined her face, her eyes, looking for the hidden meaning. "Can't complain."

She turned back toward him and leaned forward, propping her forearms on the table. "Listen, whatever you might think, I'm not in the business of railroading people—no matter who they are. And I'm pretty good at figuring out who the real culprit is."

Had she just insinuated she thought he was innocent?

"Are you always right?"

"As an investigator, so far, so good."

He noted her qualifier but chose to ignore it. Instead, he glanced toward the water and saw Thor snoozing in the sand. "Guard dog or accelerant detection?"

"Both."

"He find anything in the rubble?"

"Maybe. We'll know for sure when I get the lab report." She paused so long, Zac looked back toward her. "Why'd you give up being a firefighter?"

Hot anger hit him in the gut, as if his career—one he loved—had been stolen from him only yesterday instead of two years ago.

He snorted at her question. "You're kidding, right?"

"No. Why would I be?" She leaned back in her chair and gave him a look of challenge. "I seem to remember being a firefighter meant more than anything to you."

More than her. She didn't say the words. She didn't have to.

No matter what he'd done though, did she have to pretend?

"I wasn't hot on the idea of working with people who didn't have my back."

She scrunched her forehead.

"You seriously don't know?"

"Would I have asked you if I knew?" Irritation laced her words.

"I'm surprised you didn't hear it from your brothers."

She looked down, but not before he saw a shadow cloud her pale blue eyes. Only a moment passed before she raised her gaze and stared straight at him. "Must have slipped their minds."

Were they still estranged, even after all this time? Why did he find that surprising? He knew how unyielding the Cooke men were.

He glanced out toward the tide and let the familiar story flow out like the waves, curious how she'd react. "You'd been gone about six months when we got a call to a house fire. Turned out it was the house of a woman I'd just broken up with. Hell, it wasn't really even a breakup. We'd only gone out three or four times."

"And it was arson and the finger pointed at you?"

Zac noticed the sound of disbelief in her voice.

"Yeah. Easy target. The ex. A firefighter who understands how to make a house burn quickly. Not a native."

"All circumstantial evidence. What about the woman? What did she say?"

He snorted a mirthless half laugh. "Swore up and down I was trying to kill her. Only she wasn't at home. Though she normally would have been asleep at that time. She worked nights."

"Did the investigators have any actual hard evidence on their side?" she asked, all business.

The conversation wasn't going how Zac had expected. Where was the finger-pointing? The animosity?

"At first. They found a can of gasoline and matches in my truck, and a 'witness' said she'd heard me threaten my ex."

"Pretty damning evidence, and yet here you sit."

Randi looked down at her empty water bottle. "Why did your ex-girlfriend think you tried to kill her?"

"She was psychotic."

"Really?" Her voice rose slightly in surprise.

"I don't know if she's been diagnosed, but it's there. You don't notice at first, but that's why I broke it off." That, and the fact it had just never felt right. Not like his time with Randi had.

"And she didn't take it well."

Damn, it was odd talking to Randi about another woman.

"Obviously not. She burned her own place and tried to pin it on me."

She tilted her head a fraction. "They proved that?"

"Yeah." He watched her face, trying to figure out if she thought someone had made a mistake and he really was guilty after all. Hell, he'd strap himself to a damn lie detector machine if it'd erase this new suspicion.

"How?" She didn't sound accusatory, simply curious.

"She told a friend how she got the idea after reading about an unsolved arson in the newspaper, how she planted the evidence and got her coked-up neighbor to claim to be a witness to me threatening her. The friend told the police."

"And you didn't go back to the department after you were cleared?"

"My innocence didn't matter to a lot of people, including your family."

She crossed her arms and shifted in her seat. "They thought you did it?"

"They sure didn't back me up. Can't say I wanted to be best buddies after that."

"Why did you stay in Horizon Beach?" She stared, unwavering, at him, her captivating blue eyes making his breath catch. How could he still be attracted to her after all this time? When she could put him through the hell of suspicion again? They weren't even the same people they used to be. They didn't know each other anymore. But his body didn't seem to mind.

Randi was listening to him, wasn't she? Wasn't that more than her brothers had done?

Zac let out a sigh. "Sometimes I ask myself the same question." He stood and stalked back toward the bar. This time, he was the one who needed a drink.

RANDI WATCHED the power in Zac's movements as he zigzagged through the crowd. Heat surged to her face when she realized she was watching him in a purely I'm-still-attracted-to-him way. Only it wasn't the same as before. While he'd been young and exuberant then, now he was all man and rough around the edges. Accusation and the loss of a dream did that to a person. But why did she care? Hadn't he just received a little of his own medicine? He was no stranger to turning his back on someone he supposedly cared about.

She needed to ask Eric about the other side of Zac's story. Lord knew most of her brothers were aces at holding a grudge, but she hoped Eric would give her the honest story, one not tainted by hard feelings. It was one thing to hold a grudge when someone had done something to deserve it, quite another when they hadn't.

And she couldn't abide a wrong—even if it had been perpetrated against someone who'd once wronged her.

Someone who'd broken her heart.

Chapter Four

Randi slept badly. She wasn't sure if it was the less-than-comfortable bed, her inability to stop thinking about her family or the disturbing nightmare in which Zac was trapped inside a burning house while her brothers stood back and watched, but it didn't matter. Bad sleep was bad sleep, and Randi rolled out of bed as daylight was creeping into Horizon Beach. She changed into her running clothes and shoes, pulled her hair into a high ponytail and roused Thor. He yawned wide and tried to sneak a few more winks.

"If I have to get up at the crack of dawn, so do you."

The horizon was as pink as some of the beach homes when Randi and Thor hit the beach at a brisk jog. Thor chased shorebirds and frolicked in and out of the surf.

Gradually, the kinks in Randi's back and her headache ebbed. She'd missed running along the beach at dawn, the way the world seemed to be asleep and the day full of possibility. She sometimes managed to get over to Pensacola Beach for a morning run, but even that had become more rare as her job took her all over Florida and required increasing amounts of her time.

She wasn't complaining. Someone had to make sure

the firebugs didn't get away with their crimes. Few things were more destructive than fire. Victims lost their homes, their businesses, their very lives. Unfortunately, there were people out there whose fascination with it led to all kinds of loss—including that experienced by her father.

The latest arsonist, if indeed the Horizon Vista fire was declared arson, had put her brothers' lives at risk. So she'd be particularly happy to send him to prison.

Dissecting the case brought her thoughts back to Zac—and how he'd looked in the bar the night before. Tall, lean, corded muscles lining his strong arms. Attractive in that carefree, tanned sort of way. Maybe not so carefree. Her appearance had erased that.

When her mind focused on his physical attributes and her involuntary flushed reaction to them, she increased her pace, running instead of jogging. She ran until her muscles screamed at her to slow or move to a surface easier to run on than the packed, sloping sand. She ignored the plea, instead pushing harder. Her strides eventually brought her to the scene of the crime, causing her to slow then stop.

She stared at the hulking, black frame of Oldham's building, the suspect list running through her mind. Slowly, she circled the building, looking for anything she might have missed in her initial survey. She completed the circle empty-handed, finding herself on the side next to Zac's bar.

Despite her gut feeling that Zac couldn't be the arsonist, she'd have to thoroughly investigate the possibility. She'd depended on Cooke instinct once and it had cost her father the use of his legs and her the comfort and closeness of her family.

But when she officially cleared Zac, then what? Would she be tempted to act on her attraction? After his failure to stand up for her following the fire that had injured her father, how could she even consider that? Because part of her didn't want to hold a grudge like other members of her family, no matter how hard it would be to trust him again.

She spent the next several hours interviewing potential witnesses, including the owner of the hotel behind Zac's bar. Her instinctual belief in Zac's innocence took a hit when the man said he couldn't imagine Zac burning down Oldham's condos, but that it was possible. Then he mentioned the old arson charge, even though Zac had been cleared of that. How often was she going to encounter that prejudice?

But no matter how she tried, she couldn't believe Zac could be guilty. Zac had been a good firefighter, working as hard as the rest of them. She didn't rely on instinct anymore. It made her nervous that she did now, believing Zac had nothing to do with the fire. She refused to think about being wrong.

ZAC THREW a line into the water, hoping a little fishing would distract him. Since Randi had shown up, any chance at peace of mind had vanished.

The first time he'd ever seen her, she'd been dressed in a little pink dress and on her way to a wedding. He'd been stunned into silence. Even when he'd later seen her sweaty and wearing dirty turnout gear, she'd still been pretty. He'd pursued her until she'd finally caved and agreed to go out with him.

He sighed. That bright, fun Randi didn't seem to exist anymore. But while the years since her father's accident might have hardened her, she was even more beautiful than before, damn it.

He watched as a couple of fishing vessels motored out to sea. The sky was blindingly blue, making the water the gorgeous blue-green that attracted vacationers to the Gulf Coast. If he'd left Horizon Beach after his first brush with arson accusations, he wouldn't have had to deal with Randi Cooke or Bud Oldham, but then he'd miss mornings and views like this.

Zac glanced toward shore, where Adam lounged in his concession shack reading the latest issue of *Sports Illustrated.* To think that only a couple of days before, Zac's life had been similarly carefree. Now, he spent the hours he wasn't working or sleeping following in Randi's footsteps, doing his own investigation. Asking witnesses what they had seen, finding out all he could about Bud Oldham. The sooner the real arsonist was caught, the sooner he could go back to his normal life, free of suspicion and frustrating feelings about Randi Cooke.

Movement at the beach end of the pier drew his attention. Randi stepped onto the pier, Thor at her side, and walked over to where Adam sat. Zac resisted the urge to jump into the water to avoid her and his mentally impaired desire to kiss her. He tried to ignore her, but found himself glancing toward her and Adam every few seconds. Was she asking Adam about the fire, about him? Or was he being paranoid?

The minutes crept by, Zac feeling trapped at the end of the pier and hating himself for the reaction. Why couldn't he just walk by Randi as if he'd never seen her before? Acting as if he wasn't concerned by her presence would be the best plan.

While he was looking back to where she stood in full investigative mode, something tugged on his line. The jerk surprised him, and he almost lost hold of his fishing pole. He reeled in the line, bringing the fish toward the surface, causing it to splash the water in a vain effort to get away. After a few minutes of wrestling, Zac pulled the flounder over the side of the pier. The large, flat, speckled fish flopped against the planking, desperate to free himself.

The fish represented some good dinners, but something about the crazed, trapped look in its eyes made Zac pause. He knew exactly how the fish felt. He stooped, freed the fish from the hook then let it drop over the side of the pier.

"Didn't figure you for a catch-and-release kind of guy."

Zac didn't turn toward the sound of Randi's voice behind him. "Just goes to show you never know everything about a person, no matter how good an investigator you are."

She took a couple of steps closer. "You might be right, but it doesn't keep me from trying."

Zac stared at the waves lapping at the pier. "That I don't doubt."

"In the interest of officially removing yourself from the suspect list, why don't you help me out a bit? Did you find anything useful during your investigation yet?"

So she knew. The good ol' Horizon Beach gossip mill at work.

Zac shrugged. "Not really. Could be anyone, granted you've determined it's arson."

"So no one stands out from the crowd?"

She seemed genuinely interested, despite his defensive attitude. But it was her job to investigate every possibility. He didn't keep track of the locals like he used to. Most of his contact was with tourists and any residents who ventured into the Beach Bum.

He didn't really have close connections with anyone despite the time he'd lived there. The few friendships he'd begun to build after moving to Horizon Beach had collapsed the minute the "evidence" pointed at him two years before. Adam was the only person he could call a good friend here, though he had regular customers and neighbors with whom he enjoyed talking. Now that he looked at it like that, it seemed crazy to stay. But something about this slice of coastline had kept him from selling his home and moving on. At first, part of that reason had been a hope that Randi would return and he'd find a way to apologize. That, plus he was stubborn and didn't like being pushed around.

"No one in particular. There was a general dislike of the guy and the project. You could probably find a so-called motive for about three-quarters of the residents. People like it to stay the same here, and a fifteen-story building didn't really fit in."

"It's hard to stop change sometimes."

Zac glanced toward the burned building. "Looks like someone decided you could."

Randi didn't look at the building. Instead, she kept staring at Zac. He let the silence sit there like an unwanted guest. But instead of giving in and asking other questions, Randi didn't lose her focus.

Zac turned his gaze slowly toward Randi when he sensed her continued stare. "You've turned into a tough cookie, haven't you?"

"Some would say so." This morning, she hid her emotions so well that he couldn't tell whether she considered it a compliment or whether she was remembering how people like him had forced her to harden herself.

"I'm betting some of those are sitting in prison with arson convictions hanging around their necks."

Randi walked to the end of the pier and leaned back against the railing. "You'd win that bet."

Zac watched her, wary but also missing the little T-shirt she'd worn the night before. "I'm not planning on joining them, particularly since I'm innocent."

"Don't worry. I've never sent an innocent man to prison."

"You sure of that?"

She didn't flinch from his stare or question. "Positive."

"You're definitely a Cooke."

Her expression tightened. "And by that you mean?"

"So sure you can't be wrong." Zac took a step toward Randi but stopped when Thor sprang to attention at her side, evidently ready to chomp off an appendage with his powerful jaws if necessary. "Everyone is wrong at some point."

Her gaze caught his, and unspoken words about the past swirled between them. He nearly told her he was sorry for siding with her brothers, for saying her going into that fire had led to her father's catastrophic injury, but enough arrogant Cooke flared in those blue eyes to raise his hackles.

"Just make sure you're the only one you hurt when you're so sure," he said.

"That's rich, coming from you."

There it was, a hint of the hurt that resided below her steely, distant exterior. Damn it if his feelings didn't soften a little.

"Like I said, everyone's wrong at some point."

Zac grabbed his fishing rod and walked the length of

the pier toward the parking lot. If he didn't get away from Randi, he was going to do something crazy like pull her into his arms. He didn't have that right anymore. And even if she didn't consider him a suspect in the fire, he doubted her belief in him extended an inch beyond that. As he left her behind, the thought hurt. He deserved the pain.

RANDI WATCHED as Zac walked away, stunned by what had sounded halfway like an apology for how he'd treated her before. But his command that she should be certain she didn't hurt someone when she was wrong had brought guilt and pain to the surface, emotions she needed tucked well away while she worked. It felt incredibly wrong to have those feelings while also appreciating the mighty nice picture he painted as he walked away in worn jeans and a T-shirt that had seen approximately eight billion washings. And the resurgence of feelings more serious than simple attraction didn't help.

The old wound she'd thought long buried felt raw against snippets of their time together—walks on the beach, flirtatious whispers to each other at the fire station, the night she'd finally felt comfortable enough to make love with him. Their lovemaking had still filled her senses when they'd been called to that fateful fire. Her heart ached when she remembered how he'd looked at her afterward—with anger and accusation.

He didn't look back at her now as he got into his Jeep and drove away. Why did her heart still go crazy when she was around him, and after he'd broken it? She had to make herself forget he was anything other than a person of interest in her investigation. One she wanted to officially clear so she could avoid him.

Still standing on the end of the pier, she dialed Eric.

"Hey, what's up?" he answered.

"Tell me everything you know about when Zac Parker was accused of arson."

"Why?"

"Bud Oldham has fingered him as a potential suspect in the Horizon Vista fire."

Eric muttered an expletive.

"Nice. I bet you get all the girls with that potty mouth."

"Listen, you better be damn sure before you start even suggesting Zac had something to do with this."

"You sound like him."

"And with good reason."

"Because he was falsely accused before?"

"Yeah." The word sounded like it should be followed by even more information, but Eric didn't say anything else.

"So, it's your professional opinion that he's not a likely candidate?"

Eric sighed. "Listen, have you had breakfast?"

She frowned at his abrupt change of topic. "No."

"Meet me at Nan's." Eric hung up before she could reply. What was that all about?

It only took her five minutes to reach Nan's, a little hole-in-the-wall breakfast and lunch place popular with locals and unpopular with tourists because it didn't sit on the beach. Even with its view of the Stay Clean Carwash, it was packed.

Randi felt curious stares as she passed through the main dining room and out onto the side deck. Once, she'd been a regular here, too, but it'd been so long ago she now felt like a stranger.

She claimed the only empty table, the one in the far corner of the deck where birds liked to sit on the railing and beg for nibbles of Nan's fabulous biscuits. Thankfully, she only had to wait an uncomfortable couple of minutes before Eric showed up and slid into the plastic chair opposite her.

The waitress materialized next to them almost immediately. Once she'd taken their orders, Randi jumped right in. "So tell me why Zac Parker was a suspect in the fire two years ago."

He stared at her with a probing look. "Does this have anything to do with what happened between you two?"

"Nothing whatsoever."

"You're sure about that?"

"He made his choice. I accepted it and moved on. This is business," she said, for her own benefit as much as Eric's.

Eric didn't look totally convinced. Hell, she wasn't totally convinced. It wasn't revenge she sought, as Eric might suspect. She wanted proof that Zac wasn't guilty, but she needed to keep that to herself. She couldn't let Zac know she might still harbor feelings for him. She couldn't risk having him tromp on her heart again. After all, it was abundantly clear that she'd cared more for him than he had for her.

Eric sighed. "His ex-girlfriend made an accusation to get back at him."

"She admitted this?"

"Yes, to a friend, who told the police."

"That's what Zac said. If it was that clear-cut, why isn't he still with the department?"

"He decided to quit." Eric took a long drink of his orange juice and avoided eye contact.

She was sure she knew the answer, but she needed to hear it from her brother. "Why?"

Eric leaned back in his chair. "Think about it. Horizon Beach is small. Even with his name being cleared, there's still the taint there. The firefighter accused of setting a fire. People worry that maybe there was at least something wrong going on for him to even be accused."

Randi didn't argue. Very rarely was a truly squeaky-clean person accused of a major crime. Still, she was disappointed that even Eric hadn't admitted what she was sure had occurred—the Cookes closing ranks against one of their own.

"Do you think he's capable of setting a large fire?" *Please say no.*

Eric's eyes widened. "You mean do I think he set the Horizon Vista one? What would be the reason?"

She told him about the argument between Zac and Oldham.

"Seems excessive as payback."

She put on her devil's advocate hat. "Depends on how bad the argument was."

Eric shooed away some of the begging birds and leaned back. "From what I hear, Oldham has a whole slew of people who hate him as much or more than Zac does. Just be positive before you make any public accusations."

"Funny, Zac said something similar this morning. Odd how you both are of the same mind-set and yet he doesn't seem to be feeling the love for anyone with the last name Cooke."

Their biscuits and gravy arrived. They each took a few bites. Randi savored the warm, flaky biscuits and figured biscuits in heaven would have to taste like Nan's.

Since Eric evidently wasn't going to address Zac's falling-out with the department, Randi attacked the topic directly. "So why the animosity from Zac toward our family? Last time I saw him, he was your new best friend."

"Do you need to ask?"

As a rule, the Cooke men were the picture of firefighter solidarity, but there were times when their firefighter brethren were driven from the pack. She knew that firsthand, so why did it surprise her that Zac may have suffered the same fate? Randi stared down at her half-eaten breakfast, pushed the plate to the side of the table. She pulled enough money from her wallet for the meal and slid the bills under the edge of the plate.

"At least when I incurred the wrath, I'd actually made a mistake. Be careful or you won't have anyone at the department whose last name isn't Cooke."

She watched Eric take a bite, his body tense. She sighed. Why did she think her words would make any difference?

Randi stood. "Let me know if you hear anything."

Eric leaned his forearms on the edge of the table. "Zac is a good guy who got a raw deal. And he lost his career because of it." Eric stared at her, driving home his point that she should know better than anyone else how that felt. "I'm sorry I had any part of it."

She couldn't be sure, but perhaps that was meant for her, too.

Chapter Five

National Park Ranger James Warner was neither more nor less a suspect by the time Randi completed her interview. He had motive—vocal opposition to encroaching development near the park—but the opportunity wasn't solid. Why couldn't the arsonist in this case just hold up a blinking, neon "Guilty" sign and make her life easier? So she could get out of Horizon Beach.

On her drive back from the national seashore ranger station, her thoughts wandered away from Warner and back to Zac. She needed to do more footwork in her quest to declare him innocent of any fire involvement. As was annoyingly typical when thinking about him, her imagination and libido staged a coup. She tried remembering him in sooty turnout gear, but damned if that didn't make him seem hotter.

When Randi returned to Horizon Beach, she found herself driving by the fire station, remembering the good days there before her father's injury. The station still had three bays—two for fire engines and one for an ambulance. She spotted a couple of firefighters, an EMS guy and Jack's white head. She pulled into the parking lot before she could talk herself out of it.

"Stay," she said to Thor, who looked content to do just that. She laughed at how he stretched out to cover the entire backseat.

"Funny you should come around when there's not another Cooke in sight," Jack said before he even made eye contact.

"Pure coincidence."

Jack gave her his "I'm not buying it" look. "This from the girl who doesn't believe in coincidence."

"It exists. Just don't like it sticking its nose into my cases."

"Speaking of which, how's the investigation going?"

"You mean other than the potential suspect list looking like the complete listings of the Horizon Beach phone book?" She shoved her hands in her pockets. "You heard anything?"

Jack shook his head. "Probably the same things you have. Unhappy neighbors, suspicions of everyone on that end of town."

"What about Zac Parker? You worked with him longer than I did. Do you think he's capable of something like this?" Amazing how hard it was to keep any emotion out of her voice.

Jack shrugged. "I suspect you know about his previous arrest for arson."

She nodded. "Heard the gist of it, that he was cleared."

"Yeah." Something about the tone of Jack's voice made her examine his expression closer, afraid of what she'd find.

"What?"

"I don't know, the situation was just…off. How the ex was all gung ho that he was guilty one minute then admitted she'd lied about the whole thing the next."

Dread unfurled within her. She believed Zac innocent, but compared to Jack she barely knew him. "Do you think she was coerced to change her story?"

"No idea. Setting fire to her own place seems a little extreme just to get back at a guy who dumped her."

"A woman scorned," she said, knowing such situations could produce all manner of crazy behavior.

"I guess. But be careful your past relationship doesn't cloud your judgment."

That stung. She was a professional, and as a professional she had nothing pointing to Zac more than anyone else at the moment.

Jack sank onto the bench outside the first bay door. Randi would swear she heard his bones creak.

"Seriously, why haven't you retired?"

He extended his legs. "And do what?"

She crossed her arms and gave him a "duh" look. "Fish."

"All day every day?" he asked in a tone of disbelief that she'd suggest such a thing.

"Sure. Or you could take up another hobby."

"Fire's my hobby."

"Well, that's a weird way to look at it."

"You know what I mean. I started fighting fires damn near fifty years ago in the navy, been doing it ever since. Take that away and I'm just another old man fishing my final years away."

"You're never going to be 'just another old man.'" She'd known Jack her whole life, worked with him, considered him a part of her family. There wasn't a person in Horizon Beach other than her father who knew more about fires or the people who set them. Jack and her father had been the county's unofficial arson investigators for years.

Jack emerged from his momentary melancholy and looked at her with a bit more animation. "So, how long you think it'll take to wrap this up? You've got quite the reputation to uphold."

"Too early to tell, but hopefully not too long. It's been a busy year so far, and it doesn't look like it's going to stop."

"So it's still that way, huh?" Jack asked.

"Yeah."

Jack shook his head. "Seem to be more fires all the time, more sophisticated, better cloaked."

Randi crossed her arms. "First time I've had so many potential suspects and still have it seem like the Invisible Man set the fire."

"People don't pay as much attention to what's going on around them anymore," Jack said. "Someone could set a fire right under their nose, and they wouldn't even notice."

Randi shuddered at the thought.

When the shift change rolled around, Will and Karl showed up. They acknowledged her, but not much more than that. Not wanting to stick around and bathe in familial tension, she said goodbye and returned to the car to find Thor sleeping. He opened his eyes briefly then went back to serenading her with snores.

When Randi left the fire station, she'd had a more than full day and yet didn't want to go back to her hotel room. A twitchy energy pulsed, urging her to keep looking, asking questions.

She pulled over and flipped through her notes. Zac's address caught her eye. He'd evidently moved from the apartment he'd lived in before. What would it hurt to drive by, see where he lived now? If he saw her, she could say she was checking to see if he'd heard anything new.

Zac's cottage sat at the end of a cul-de-sac. No Jeep in the gravel driveway. She should drive away and ignore her natural curiosity, but she parked and stepped out. Thor started after her as he had throughout the day.

"Stay, boy. I'll just be a minute."

Thor remained in the car but sat at attention next to the open window in case she called him.

The sun's late-afternoon glow filtered across the neighborhood, turning it a kind of magical pinkish orange like the inside of a seashell. If things hadn't happened as they had, would she be living here with Zac now? Was it possible they'd be married, maybe even have a child? She'd never know.

After a glance along the street, she walked up Zac's driveway and knocked on the door. When no one answered, she circled to the backyard. Good—no secret stash of gasoline or billboard that said, *An arsonist lives here.* Just a grill and a single lawn chair. Zac must do all his entertaining at work. An unwanted jolt of happiness zipped through her. Damn it, she was so weak where he was concerned. Had been from the moment he'd convinced her to go out with him.

She stepped up onto the concrete patio and peeked in an uncovered window. Typical small, spartan kitchen of the American male.

Thor barked, so she turned to leave. She gasped when she saw someone standing at the corner of the house. Not just someone. Zac.

"Does your job give you the right to trespass?"

Crap! Her heart rate increased at being caught snooping. Why hadn't Thor given her more warning?

"No, sorry." She glanced at the house. "I was trying to determine if you were home." Oh, that was lame.

"Seems the fact that there wasn't a vehicle in the driveway and no one answered the door would be clues," he said past the reined anger she saw in the tight stance of his body.

"How do you know I knocked?"

"Sane people would before creeping through the backyard."

"I wasn't creeping."

He gave her a look that said she was full of it.

"Someone called you, didn't they?" she asked.

"Not everyone thinks I'm itching to burn down Horizon Beach."

"I never said that." She tried her best not to sound defensive. After all, he had no idea she really wanted to clear him.

"And what does peeking in my back window say? Do you think I have a secret arson room?" he asked, as if she'd lost her mind. He moved toward her quickly, causing her to back up involuntarily. Instead of confronting her nose to nose, he passed her, unlocked the back door, let it swing open. He pointed his arm toward the interior. "Go ahead, you're so curious."

Randi swallowed past the dryness in her throat. "That's not necessary." When had she become such a brainless idiot?

"Isn't it?" he asked as he strode to within three feet of her. "I bet you're dying to dig through my stuff, look for any tiny piece of evidence that you can use to make this fire stick to me. Payback is a bitch and all that."

Okay, that was unfair. She wasn't vindictive. Randi propped her hands on her hips. "I'm not trying to pin anything on you. Not that you'll believe that."

He crossed his arms and stared at her. "You're hard to believe right now."

Damn, why hadn't she curbed her impulse to drive by his house? To nose around? "I was just going to see if you'd heard anything else."

"Yeah, right."

"Hell, you sure have turned into a hard-ass. No wonder people are wondering if you set that fire."

"Now, there's a surprise." His expression said it was anything but. "Ever thought maybe they have something to hide themselves?"

Jack's lined and timeworn face came to mind. "I seriously doubt that." At least in most of the instances.

He pointed to the side of his head. "Think about it. Everyone jumps to conclusions in situations like this. I'm an easy person to suspect because I've been charged with arson before. Doesn't matter that I didn't do it then either. The accusation is still there."

Hadn't Eric said the same thing?

Zac shook his head. "I should have moved away from you people when I had the chance."

"You people?" Her temper flickered at his accusatory tone.

"Cookes. You're all alike, always thinking the worst of people."

"That's not true!" And yet a little twinge of truth poked at her. Hadn't her family cooled even toward her? Hadn't her brothers chosen to blame her for their father's paralysis? True, it was her fault, but their distance from her tore her up inside all the same.

"No?" Zac stalked to the edge of the patio. "I didn't see any of them sticking up for me when I was charged falsely."

"What were they supposed to think?" she asked, her voice rising. "There was physical evidence." Despite their faults, she had to defend her family.

Zac turned toward her and pointed in her direction. "That's the problem. They didn't think. They took the accusation at face value and didn't even ask me if I'd done it."

If that was true, she didn't blame him for being angry. Hadn't her family's gut-instinct-now, ask-questions-later mentality been what had led her into the fire that injured her dad? Still, she played devil's advocate out of habit. "How many arsonists are going to admit it? My family still didn't know you well."

"They know you well. What's your excuse?"

He might as well have punched her in the stomach. For a couple of stunned seconds while she tried to catch her breath, she just looked at him, not believing what he'd said. Randi stalked past him toward her car only to find it blocked by Zac's Jeep.

"Listen—"

Randi held up her hand. "Don't." She nodded toward the Jeep. "Move it or I'm driving through your front yard."

Angry tears popped into her eyes, making her even angrier. She wrenched the door of her car open and sank into the seat before slamming the door. She ignored Thor's whine and refused to make eye contact with Zac, who stood outside the driver's side of her car, his palms propped on the door frame so he could lean down to her level. Hoping to prompt him into action, she started the engine.

Finally, he moved his Jeep. She wanted to slam on the accelerator and speed away. Instead, she backed from the driveway and drove down the street at normal speed, without even looking at Zac. Should she turn this case over to another investigator? On top of it being frustrating, it was opening old wounds, ones that had never completely healed.

But to do so would be to admit she couldn't handle the situation. And she was determined that no one would ever say that about her—no matter what personal minefields she had to navigate.

ZAC STOOD by the Jeep and watched Randi drive away with her jaw set so tight he feared it might crack. He'd hit a sore spot he'd suspected still existed since their talk at the bar, and he'd meant to. But instead of making him feel better, he felt juvenile and petty. And like a total ass for throwing the worst event of her life in her face.

He knew she was only doing her job, but he was damned tired of being the guy everyone assumed was burning stuff down. He knew she was investigating other leads. Word was she was interviewing everyone who moved.

His own investigation was turning up no clear answers, either, just lots of maybes. Not too damn useful when trying to clear your name and erase any hint of doubt on the face of a woman who occupied way too much of your thoughts.

RANDI STARTED the next day with a longer, harder run than usual. Running kept her in shape. Normally it helped clear her thoughts, but it wasn't working so well this morning. She still couldn't rid her memory of what

Zac had said and why it had mattered so much. Because he had to know how much it had hurt her. He'd been part of that pain.

But you were snooping around his house.

She slowed, stopped, sucked air into her heaving lungs. Of course he'd assumed the worst. What kind of sense did it make that her poking around was because of her curiosity about his life now and not suspicion about the fire? Until she solved this case, she needed to steer clear of Zac unless she had to talk to him for professional reasons. He caused her brain to short-circuit.

The jog back to the hotel allowed Randi time to fantasize about Zac in a safe environment, meaning he was nowhere near her. She needed to get it all out now in case she ran into him again and had to be cool and distant. Hard to do when the sight of him made her think about a huge white bed, the ocean breeze blowing through sheer curtains and mind-blowing sex.

She'd replayed their one night together endless times in the months after the fire, while she was alone and miserable in a new town. She'd allowed herself the memory of his fingers on her skin, the taste of his mouth, the hardness of his body beside hers. Eventually, she'd forced herself to stop because it hurt too much to remember.

She refocused on the day ahead—people to interview, a check-in with the office, more surveillance tape to watch. As she rounded the corner of her hotel, she spotted a familiar yellow Jeep and halted. So much for avoiding Zac.

He leaned against the front of the Jeep, arms crossed. A dream from the previous night, one she'd forgotten, popped to the front of her brain. After what he'd said to her, she'd still dreamed about caressing his bare chest over and over, feeling his heartbeat beneath her hands.

Zac caught sight of her and walked toward her.

Great. She looked anything but attractive—or even professional—at the moment. But she wasn't about to avoid him and let him know how much his presence bothered her. So she walked toward him as she wiped the sweaty hair away from her forehead.

"You okay?" he asked.

"Yeah. Why wouldn't I be?" Did he think she was still upset over their previous encounter? Well, yes, but she wasn't going to let him know that.

He pointed toward her car, which had a flat back tire.

"I must have run over something."

"I don't think you ran over something." He walked toward the car and she followed.

As Randi got closer, she saw what he meant. Not one, not two, no, all four tires were flat to the rims. "Somebody punctured my tires." She looked back at Zac.

"Oh, come on. If I'd done it, would I be standing here?"

"I didn't say you did anything. I didn't even think it." And she hadn't. "Stop assuming you know what I'm thinking."

Zac redirected his gaze to her car. "Looks like you're getting closer to identifying the arsonist, and he doesn't like it."

She ran her hand over her sweaty hair. Her suspect list ran through her head. Some she eliminated because they weren't physically capable of puncturing car tires. But a handful were, including Oldham. Zac was physically able to do such damage, but like he said, why would he stick around?

She'd have to verify where they all were last night. She glanced at her watch. "Damn, I've got a meeting in forty-five minutes."

"Where do you have to go?"

"The courthouse."

"I'll drop you off."

Randi eyed Zac. "Didn't expect that offer." The fact they were even standing within a few feet of each other hit her. "Why are you here, anyway?"

Zac sighed. "Because I made a low blow yesterday and I'm trying to make up for it."

"Fine. A truce," she said.

"I can live with that."

The softening of the tension in his face let more of his good looks come out. Her heart fluttered in response. Ignoring it, she gestured toward her ruined tires. "I'd better go call someone to come fix this." She headed for the stairs up to her second-floor hotel room.

"Randi."

She halted and looked back at him. "Yeah?"

"You should call the cops, too."

Her heart squeezed at what sounded like genuine concern. "You're probably right."

"I know I am." He stared at her, determined and serious. "If you're getting close and the person is trying to scare you off, his actions might escalate."

She tried to lighten the mood by relaxing her tight posture and almost smiling. "When did you become an expert on the criminal mind?"

"Just common sense. If he doesn't want to be found out, he'll likely do whatever he can to prevent it."

Despite her warm body temperature, a chill zipped along her spine. Some arsonists just liked to burn things.

Others didn't mind taking a few human lives in the process.

"I'll call them. And thanks for the ride offer, but it's not necessary."

Zac sighed. "So much for the truce." He turned and walked toward his Jeep before she could respond. What could she say, anyway? That she was declining the offer because spending time with him just made her long for things that weren't meant to be? After all, it wasn't as if they were going to pick up their relationship where they'd left off before the fire that had caused so many splits.

After showering and changing, she called the police and reported the incident, telling them she would take pictures and drop them by so they didn't have to send out an officer. Then she went to the hotel office and told the manager what had happened and inquired about the security video from the night before. Maybe she'd have more luck with this one than that from the hotel next to the condos.

"Well, it depends on what time it happened. One of the housekeeping ladies found a T-shirt hanging over the camera this morning. Idiot night clerk must have never looked at the video." He motioned her into his office. "What time would you like to start at?"

"About eight o'clock." Her car had still been fine then.

Randi watched, fast-forwarded, watched some more… until the camera suddenly was covered at 2:13 a.m.

The hotel manager returned to the office doorway from the front desk when he heard her click off the video.

"Do you still have the shirt?" she asked.

He pointed toward a wadded-up T-shirt on his desk.

She picked it up at the edges and let it unfurl. Printed on the shirt above a bright cartoon design was "Cinco de Mayo at the Beach Bum, May 2005."

Zac's earlier words came back. It looked like somebody was setting him up for the fall.

Chapter Six

Darla Finnegan eyed Zac from her position behind her desk at the Horizon Beach Chamber of Commerce. He normally saw her in casual clothes when she and her husband, Kevin, stopped by the bar for a drink on Friday evenings. Today, however, her long, dark hair was pulled up and she wore a tan pantsuit. Both conveyed the professionalism her position as chamber president required.

"No, I don't know of any other developers interested in the area," she said in response to his question.

"No one who'd be threatened by Oldham's resort?" Zac asked as he paced.

She shook her head. "Why are you asking these questions? You haven't gone back to the fire department, have you?"

"No. Just interested."

"Because Randi Cooke has been here already, asking similar questions."

Zac sank back in his chair. "When?"

"This morning."

Must have been the appointment she'd mentioned. "Guess she's already been across the hall, too?"

"Yeah, she visited the police first. Randi doesn't think it might be you, does she?"

"Oldham named me as a potential suspect."

"Why?"

"I might have told him to go screw himself."

Darla rolled her eyes. "Oh yeah, that's smart."

"He ticked me off."

"Men." Darla shook her head. "Who hasn't he ticked off?"

"That's the problem. Could be anybody."

"Well, at least Randi has a few more likely suspects than you."

"Did she say who?"

"Not to me, but this building is so old the walls have ears." Darla smiled.

"No doubt those ears are attached to your sister."

April Daniels worked as a dispatcher for the police department. Zac had gone out with her a couple of times before she met and fell hard for Mike Daniels. It was just as well. He'd still been all tied up in thoughts of Randi at that time.

"You are correct. Seems Randi is also interested in James Warner, the head ranger out at the Seashore, and someone else April didn't catch because a 911 call came in."

Zac smiled, and it felt foreign, considering he'd not had much to smile about lately. "Thanks."

"You bet. I expect a round on the house this Friday," she said as she shook her finger at him.

"You got it." He stood.

"Be careful, okay?" She flattened her hands against the top of her desk and looked more serious.

He gave her a grateful smile. "Don't worry. I'll be there to serve the drinks Friday."

After looking up the Seashore's number in the phone book provided by Darla's secretary, Zac left the building while dialing his cell.

"Gulf Islands National Seashore," a woman answered.

"James Warner, please."

"He's not in. Would you like to leave a message?"

Zac paused, considered, then went with his gut. "No. I was just wanting to confirm our one-o'clock-meeting location."

The sound of riffling paper came over the phone. "There must be an error on the schedule. He's not due back from the rally until three."

Rally? Think quickly. An item from that morning's news clicked in his memory. "My mistake. I must have the wrong day. Sorry." He hung up before the woman realized he was lying. He called Suz and told her he'd be late. He should go to work, but the need to prove to everyone in this town that he was innocent compelled him to keep digging. The thought of people like Randi's family looking at him with suspicion ate at him. And he didn't need them filling Randi's head with doubts about him when she could really make his life difficult. He wanted his name cleared for good.

Thirty minutes later, he arrived at a protest of a new housing development in nearby Coral Shores. Green Brigade picketers walked back and forth, blocking the entrance of earthmoving equipment to what the group considered a fragile wetland. Another member shouted through a bullhorn, "Hell no, we won't go!"

He was all for protecting Mother Nature when possible, but these people were freaking nuts to go to such extremes to make a point. And the ones who showed their faces weren't the worst of them. The visible people didn't usually resort to violence, but there were others who were never seen but often left destruction in their wake. They claimed responsibility for shooting out the windows of construction companies, sledgehammering SUVs in car lots, and even burning down the homes of developers. The burning of the Horizon Vista Resort was just their style.

Zac scanned the crowd but didn't spot Warner. Of course, he'd only seen the man's picture in the paper and might not recognize him in person. He stood back and listened to the vitriol for a few minutes before he identified the leader of the group. When the middle-aged woman relinquished the bullhorn to the next person, Zac headed for her. Maybe someone else here was the culprit and finding Warner wasn't necessary. How likely was it that a national park ranger had resorted to arson, anyway?

"You're pretty adamant about this project not going forward," Zac said as he came up next to the woman.

She glanced over at him, sizing him up. "It's past time people realize the earth can only take so much abuse."

"People have to have somewhere to live."

"So do the creatures who call this wetland home. They can't pick up and move to a condo on the beach."

"Funny you should mention condos on the beach. You wouldn't happen to know anything about the fire that destroyed the Horizon Vista Resort, would you?"

She smiled, satisfaction spreading across her face. "I know whoever did it is a hero."

Zac bit down on his instinctive response that she was a loon. "That a fact? This person have a name?"

"Do you?"

"Let's call me an interested party."

The woman took a sheet of paper from one of her colleagues. She glanced at it as she continued walking and talking. "Do you have a badge, Mr. Interested Party?"

"I'm not a cop, not an official of any kind."

The woman finally stopped walking and turned to face him. She crossed her arms. "Then what's your interest?"

Zac considered lying, but he hoped if he told the truth the woman might be inclined to do the same. "There's a woman from the state fire marshal's office investigating the fire, and she's been told I could be a suspect."

The woman raised her eyebrows. "Should you be?"

"No," he snapped.

She stared at him for a moment. "I believe you."

Zac shoved his hands in his pockets. "That's a first."

"And now I need you to believe me. While I admire the work, we had nothing to do with it."

He nodded toward the crowd. "What about some of the people in your group who've done some of the, let's say, bigger stuff?"

"When I say we, I mean the entire organization. We're kept very well informed about what is going on nationwide. Green Brigade, unfortunately, had nothing to do with that fire."

"You're positive?"

"Have you ever known us to miss the opportunity to take credit for something that big?"

Granted, he wasn't too up on his militant environmental groups, but what she said had the ring of truth. Even if many members of the organization deserved to sit behind bars for other reasons.

He sighed in irritation. "Well, I guess that leaves me back at square one."

"Good luck in your hunt. When you find the person, tell them we are most impressed."

Enough of his former firefighting self remained for Zac to have to fight saying something ugly. "A tip…" He pointed toward the picketers and the wetland area. "You might attract more flies with honey than vinegar." Sure his words would not have the desired effect, he turned and headed back to his Jeep, feeling as though he'd wasted half a day. As he opened his driver's-side door, a familiar car sporting four new tires pulled up beside him. Randi got out and stared at him.

"Fancy meeting you here," she said. "You a closet environmentalist?"

"Not particularly."

"Then why are you at the rally of a group with a record of violent, destructive behavior?" She crossed her arms and pinned him with a curious gaze. Not accusatory, just curious.

Zac leaned one palm against the Jeep. "As a matter of fact, I'm helping you do your job."

"Really?" She gave him one of those annoying half-amused expressions. It reminded him of what she used to look like when she really smiled, and that memory gave him an unexpected kick in the gut. He was part of the reason that smile was on the endangered species list.

"Yes. Figured one of this bunch might have a beef with Oldham."

"And did your fine detection skills find out anything?"

"This group had nothing to do with the fire."

"And you figured this out how?"

"I asked their leader. She said no."

Randi shook her head as if he were a naive child. "And you believed her? You ought to know arsonists don't admit their crimes simply because someone asked if they did it."

"This group likes headlines when they do something big. No glory in keeping it quiet."

Randi didn't have a comeback, so he figured he'd finally hit on something that made sense to her analytical mind. But the pause didn't last long.

"As it happens, I was looking for you anyway, though I didn't think I'd find you here," Randi said.

"What now?"

The hardness in the stance of this new Randi lessened as she reached inside the car and grabbed something. She rounded the front of her car, unfurled a T-shirt in front of her. "Recognize this?"

He stared at the shirt, puzzled by her question. "Yeah. It's a shirt we had made for Cinco de Mayo. The bar is really busy that day."

"Guess where I found it."

He shrugged. "A yard sale maybe."

"Try again."

He exhaled in frustration. "I have no idea, but I'm sure you're going to enlighten me."

"It was draped over the hotel parking lot surveillance camera last night so there is no visual of my tires being punctured."

Anger surged through him. "This is serious. Did you call the police?" His hands clenched at the idea of her being hurt by a desperate criminal.

"Yes. I think you're right about someone trying to frame you."

"You believe me?"

She held up the shirt with one hand. "You're not this stupid or obvious. Someone who knows about the fake charge against you from before is trying to use it to deflect suspicion away from himself."

"He's not only trying to frame me, but also threatening you. This isn't your run-of-the-mill fire starter."

She returned his gaze, barely blinking. "Surprisingly enough, I figured that much out on my own."

His tensed muscles relaxed at her revelation. He stared back into her bright blue eyes, stunned by how good it felt to have her believe him. It hadn't fully hit him until now how much it had bothered him that she might not. "Glad you finally saw the light," he said, half-jokingly.

She balled up the T-shirt and tossed it over Thor's head through the open car window. "My job is to build a case using facts, evidence. I come onto a case where the victim had a public altercation with a potential suspect, a guy with a past arson charge, what am I supposed to think?"

"Don't think for a minute. Go with your gut."

She stiffened and took a couple of steps away from him. "I'm not a go-with-your-gut kind of gal. Not anymore."

Damn. He always seemed to say the wrong thing around her. One of these decades he was going to learn to think before he opened his mouth.

"I'm not saying to ignore the evidence. We're both going around Horizon Beach asking the same questions of the same people. We should join forces, get this case solved as soon as possible."

"I'll think about it."

"Don't think too long."

"I usually work only with Thor. And even though I believe you, I don't have proof yet. I have to be careful with appearances. When people look at me, they have to see impartiality."

"Well, when people look at me, I want them to stop seeing the damn Human Torch."

RANDI AWOKE the next morning, her first thought of the dream she'd had before waking, one in which Zac had been kissing her brainless. The flush and arousal lingered as she woke more fully. She shook her head. Just being near the man made her want to do things that had nothing to do with finding an arsonist.

She focused her thoughts on the case while out for her morning run, but when she returned to the room and stripped off her sweaty clothes, images of Zac planted themselves front and center. What was she, fifteen and hormonal?

When Randi stepped into the shower, her thoughts veered only slightly to the suggestion Zac had made the day before, that they should work together. Considering her lust and the fact he was still technically a suspect to the outside world, it was a very bad idea. But as she worked the shampoo into her hair, she seriously considered the pros of the idea. What if she did bring Zac on board? He might have some insights about fire behavior that could prove useful. And he was likely more knowledgeable about the goings-on of Horizon Beach than she was now.

She hated to admit it, but the idea had merit. She'd just have to stay focused on their common goal and not how dangerously attracted she was to him. And he'd have to agree to her facts-only methods. No assumptions allowed. She'd let him know her decision when she happened to bump into him. She certainly wasn't going to seek him out. She needed more time to get used to the idea of working side by side with him without letting her unwise feelings show.

Following another fruitless morning of beating the proverbial bushes, Randi was on the verge of believing she was stuck in a nightmare and there'd actually never been a condo fire.

After ending a call to her office, Randi drove up and down streets, her hands clenching and unclenching on the wheel as frustration threatened to suffocate her. She pulled over at McGovern Park, the only public parking area in town where she could see the Gulf without having to climb over the dunes.

What next? And what if the real perp was someone she hadn't even identified as a possibility so far? That thought made her brain ache.

Why would a person burn down a condo high-rise? Money, revenge and, her least favorite, a random act. The latter was by far the hardest to solve, and this case was already difficult enough without adding that pain. Okay, she needed to backtrack, start at the beginning to see if she'd overlooked anything pointing to anyone in particular.

The beginning. She sighed then pulled her car from the parking lot.

When she arrived at the fire station, Jack's vehicle wasn't there. But Will, Karl and Josh were on duty. Great, the three brothers most likely not to want to see her. Will noticed her first and tried to retreat to the office. Her anger rose so quickly she yelled at him. "Will! I need to talk to you." Nervous looks passed between Karl and Josh. Even D. J. Watts, who'd joined the department about a month before she left, looked a little twitchy.

Will stopped, turned and crossed his arms. "Yeah?"

Deliberately, she walked over to where her other brothers were sitting around a card table playing poker with D.J. She sank onto the running board of the Number 2 engine. Thor sat next to her, as alert as if he were doing the interview. "I need to talk to you about the Horizon Vista fire."

"I've already told you all we know."

Will's quick dismissal made her lose her grip on her temper. "What, you're the eyes, ears and brain for everyone now?"

Will's jaw tightened.

Damn. She knew Will had always been closest to their father, had been the most vocal about her not putting herself and others in harm's way. She could still hear him yelling her name as she'd rushed toward the biggest mistake of her life. But she didn't even recognize him anymore. He went above and beyond the call of making her relive that horrible day.

"Oh, sit down and stop looking like you're going to explode," she said, likely infuriating him further. "I'm not here to convince you to suddenly like me again."

Karl and Josh looked like they wanted to flee to Canada.

"Leave the personal stuff out of it," Will said.

"Gladly," she bit out. "Now, I need to know if you all have heard anything, or saw anything the night of the fire that was suspicious. Anyone hanging around who wouldn't have normally been there? A comment that seemed out of the ordinary. Anything at all that might help." She hated feeling inept in front of Will, but if it helped solve the case, so be it.

Nearly as one, they shook their heads.

"See, you already know everything we do. You seem to think we're hiding something from you," Will said.

Randi took a deep breath, trying to remain calm. "Sorry. This case is making me damned cranky." She propped her forearms on her thighs and leaned forward.

"I thought Zac Parker was the main suspect," D.J. said.

How quickly public opinion had converted Zac from potential suspect to primary suspect. No wonder he was as eager to solve this case as she was. "Everything is circumstantial at best, and it may be that whoever is responsible is trying to pin the crime on Zac because of his previous charge."

"Is that how he explained it?" Will didn't even try to hide his derision.

Randi caught and held her older brother's gaze. "That's what my investigation has determined. Believe it or not, I know what I'm doing."

The veins in Will's neck became more pronounced as he appeared to hold back words Randi was sure she didn't want to hear. She shook her head and returned her attention to the other men.

A few more minutes of talking about the specifics of the fire and its aftermath yielded nothing useful. Randi stood, saying she'd be questioning the other firefighters who'd worked the fire, including those who came in from other districts. She was tired just thinking about it. The thought of having help was looking better by the minute. Her cell phone rang as she was about to leave. She flipped it open. "Randi Cooke."

"You up for some lunch?" Zac asked.

She wasn't hungry, but she liked the idea of having lunch with Zac just because it would tick off Will if he knew. She tried not to acknowledge the faster beating of her heart.

"Meet me at the Ocean Grille in fifteen minutes." She barely heard his "okay" as her attention was drawn by Will walking outside. She clicked her phone shut. With a deep sigh that stretched back three years, she walked out and stood beside her oldest brother without looking at him. "You know, once upon a time you actually liked me." She paused, but he didn't respond. "I miss that." And then she left.

Will didn't call after her, didn't ask her to forgive him for pushing her out of the family, for obviously thinking she was still so mentally deficient that she was making another huge mistake. It didn't matter how successful she was in her job, Will was always going to see her as a failure, as the reason their father would never walk again.

THE STRAIN in Randi's voice over the phone had suggested something was wrong, but Zac knew it the moment he saw her face. When she spotted him, she made a valiant effort to hide her true feelings, but it was too late. He'd already seen.

"What's wrong?" he asked when she slid into the booth opposite him.

She waved her hand. "Nothing, just some sibling stuff."

So, her brothers again. Hadn't they done enough to Randi? Hadn't he?

She grabbed a menu. "So, why the call for lunch?"

He wanted to question her further, to find out what her brothers had done to upset her, but he figured if he shared some information with her she might loosen up and confide in him. Okay, maybe that was hoping for a lot.

"I have a friend who works at the *Tampa Tribune*. I

had her dig around in their archives to see if there was anything interesting about Oldham that might indicate he had real enemies."

"You think someone might have come up here from Tampa to burn down his building?"

He made his meal selection then set aside the menu. "I don't know, but it doesn't hurt to check it out."

"Find out anything?"

"I'm not the first person he's tried to bully into selling to him. One guy even filed a harassment charge against him, but it was dropped."

"Does your friend know why?"

Zac shrugged. "No, but she's going to do a little more digging, might go talk to the guy who made the charge."

"She? Wonder if it's anyone I've met while working down there."

Zac resisted the urge to smile. Maybe she didn't hate him after all. "Emily Jasper. And yes, she's an old girlfriend, from when we both lived in Tallahassee."

Randi gave him a sideways look as she scanned the restaurant. "I didn't ask that."

"Didn't you?"

"Why on earth would I care if she was your girlfriend?"

"Old girlfriend."

Randi made a dismissive gesture. "Whatever."

Egging Randi on was the most fun he'd had all day. It reminded him of those first days he'd been pursuing her. "I don't know. Why would you care?"

"I don't."

"Uh-huh."

Randi was on the verge of denying it again, but she clamped her mouth shut.

"I guess you think this little bit of info is helping the cause of us working together?"

"Is it working?"

She stared at him, her face unreadable. When she'd stepped into his bar the day after the condo fire, he'd thought Randi was as tough as her brothers. Now he knew different. She was tougher.

"I'd already decided to accept your help. But we keep it quiet because I don't need my boss thinking I've lost my mind. And you answer to me and we do things my way."

He looked into her unrelenting blue eyes, actually stunned she'd agreed. Stunned but pleased. "Deal."

They said nothing as the waitress took their orders. After Randi handed over her menu, she stared out the open window at the surf washing onto the beach filled with sun lovers.

Zac admired her profile. Her long, blond ponytail hung down her back. Her skin glowed with health and only the slightest hint of makeup. He liked that, a woman confident enough that she didn't have to hide under layers of falseness. And yet behind all her confidence, he sensed a vulnerability she no doubt would deny if asked about it outright.

"What did they say to upset you?"

"What?"

"Your brothers."

She sighed. "I'm not upset, just tired. I didn't sleep well last night." She still watched the waves as if she'd never seen them before. "Thor grunted all night."

"Sounds like you need a better sleeping companion." He didn't know why he'd said it, but the comment had the effect of making her turn abruptly toward him.

He expected her to leave or tell him he was an ass, but she shocked him.

"Is that an offer?" Her eyes held challenge as she refused to look away.

He leaned forward, an unexpected smile tugging on his lips. "Would you take it?"

Man, this was so not the direction in which he thought this conversation was going to head. And then he got it. She wasn't flirting because she was still attracted to him.

"Oh, very good attempt at changing the subject."

She didn't deny it, merely took a sip of her water.

"I know the kinds of unyielding hard-asses your brothers can be. Once they make up their minds, it's like trying to move a continent to change them. I guess we've both experienced that."

Randi ran her finger up and down through the condensation on her glass. "Some things will just never change."

"But some will." Zac took a deep breath. "I'm sorry about before. I didn't behave any better than they did after your dad was hurt."

"Why did you do it?" she asked on a tired sigh mixed with the old hurt.

He leaned his head back and looked at the ceiling. Should he tell her? He'd wanted to in the weeks after she'd left Horizon Beach, after he'd had time to think about how stupid he'd been and how much he'd lost. But he hadn't been able to find her to apologize, to explain his knee-jerk reaction. He let out a long, slow breath.

"My dad was completely worthless, lazy. He got fired from every job he ever held. Finally, he got caught selling cocaine outside my school, went to prison and managed to get himself killed. I didn't want to be a loser like him, didn't want anyone to ever know about him." He wadded his napkin into a tight ball. "I had a good life, a good career."

"And you thought if you didn't agree with my brothers, you'd lose it all."

"That and I was so angry with you for scaring me half to death like you did by going back into that fire. I guess part of me wanted to punish you." He sighed. "It all sounds stupid now, but it made sense at the time."

They sat in silence for several endless moments.

"I'm truly sorry," he said. "I tried to find you to apologize, but you'd disappeared."

"No one knew where I was for a few months. I wanted to crawl into a hole and never come out."

"I was wrong to abandon you. My only excuse was that I was an idiot."

Randi stared at her glass. "Thank you."

"For what?"

"For the apology. It means a lot."

"I should have kept trying to find you, but time passed and—"

"And you tried to forget. I tried to do the same thing."

"I'm still sorry for how I treated you, especially now that you're giving me a chance and they never did."

Randi looked at him with more understanding than he deserved. "Did you try explaining to them?"

"Did you?"

"It was an entirely different situation."

"How so?"

She looked down at her place mat, one of those paper kind that highlighted fun facts about the Gulf Coast and Horizon Beach. "With me, they were right."

Their food arrived as he was about to tell her how wrong she was, but the moment for exploring their mistakes seemed to pass—at least for now.

Randi dived right into her shrimp po'boy. Whether she was that hungry or simply wanted to use food to end the conversation, he wasn't sure. Instinct told him not to push. They didn't talk much while they ate. When they finished, Randi wiped her mouth and threw her napkin atop her cleaned plate.

"Let me know what you hear from your friend."

"Okay."

She started to slide out of the booth.

"Randi?"

She paused and looked over at him. "Yeah?"

"You haven't had any other threats, have you?"

She shook her head, though she looked tired doing so. "I haven't really gotten any threats."

"I'd call four flat tires a threat."

She sighed. "Remember what I said about facts only? There was no note indicating it had anything to do with the investigation."

"Did there have to be?"

She slumped against the back of the booth. "No, but what am I supposed to do about it, run and hide? I have a job to do. And Thor is with me all the time. Speaking of which, I'd better get him something to eat."

Zac reached across the table and grabbed her hand. It felt so small in his and yet not fragile. "Be careful, okay?"

She stared back at him, and he saw something more in those gorgeous blue eyes. The sensation of her skin against his palm heightened. Did she feel some of the same renewed attraction?

"Randi, honey, I didn't expect to run into you today."

Randi jerked her hand out of his as she looked up at a lovely woman with blond hair like her own.

"Hey, Mom." Randi's pale complexion darkened, making her look like she'd been caught making out on the front porch. "I didn't expect to see you, either."

Mrs. Cooke looked at Zac, and he pulled a smile from somewhere. The woman had the knowing look all mothers seemed to gain the moment they gave birth. "Zac, it's nice to see you," she said in a friendly but reserved tone as she extended her hand.

Zac stared at her hand. He couldn't have been more stunned if she'd kissed him on the cheek. He clasped her hand finally and shook it. "You too, ma'am."

"I'm sorry to interrupt your lunch—"

"It's okay. I was just leaving," Randi explained.

Zac didn't like the ugly feeling her backpedaling caused in his middle. Was she ashamed that her mother might think there was something more than business between them? Was she afraid of what her brothers would say if they knew she was having lunch with him?

He caught her gaze, held it. He couldn't decipher what he saw in those eyes now, but it wasn't camaraderie or anything more affectionate. Fine. She could hide all she wanted, but damned if he would. "Yeah, we're trying to track down any out-of-town leads that might help determine who set the Horizon Vista fire."

Randi narrowed her eyes and looked like she could strangle him.

"Ah," Mrs. Cooke said as she nodded. The woman wasn't fooled. Hell, a head of cabbage would have been able to see Zac had been looking at Randi as pure woman. Not an investigator, not the sister of the men who had failed to stand behind him when he was wrongly charged. A beautiful woman who had a hurt deep inside.

A woman willing to give him a chance to prove his innocence but who didn't want to be seen with him.

Zac looked at his watch. "Well, I have to get to work." He gave Randi a cool, detached glance. "I'll call you if I find out anything." He slid from the booth and walked out of the restaurant. As he drew closer to his Jeep, he kept thinking maybe Randi would come outside, stop him, explain, apologize, something. Why did he want her to? He even looked back at the restaurant before he slipped into the driver's seat. No sign of her.

Who the hell was he kidding, anyway? She might not have him down as public enemy number one, but they weren't about to rekindle their romantic relationship, either.

No matter how attractive that option might be.

RANDI DIDN'T WATCH Zac walk away. Neither could she face her mother as she slipped into the seat Zac had vacated. What was her mom thinking? Would she tell Randi's brothers and dad about her meeting with Zac, driving an even bigger wedge between them? Randi's head ached with thinking about the extra tension that would rise up between her and the Cooke men. Not to mention the professional implications if word got out she was working with someone still considered a suspect in some people's eyes—someone with whom she'd had a sexual relationship.

"Do your brothers know about this?" Inga asked.

"No, and I'd like to keep it that way."

"Okay. You're a smart woman. I trust your judgment."

Randi looked at her mother, shocked. She couldn't believe her mother really thought that, not after her lack of judgment had cost the family so much.

Inga patted Randi's hand where it rested on the table. "Look at how many arsons you've solved. That takes brains and hard work."

Randi wanted to tell her mother how much her words meant, but she couldn't speak, half expecting to wake up from a dream.

Inga glanced at the door. "He's a nice young man. I told your father he owed him an apology, but…well, you know how difficult it is for Cooke men to swallow their pride and admit they're wrong."

"They don't think they were wrong. At least Will doesn't. He's still convinced Zac is a suspect."

"And you aren't."

"No."

"Are you two—"

"No," Randi said, interrupting her mom before she could voice the rest of the question. "He's just determined to help in the investigation."

"To clear his own name?" Inga asked.

"Yeah."

Inga smiled. "I think there's a bit more to it than that."

"What?"

Her mother's smile reached her eyes. "I'll let you figure that out." Inga checked her watch. "Gotta go, sweetie. I have a library board meeting in ten minutes."

After her mother left, Randi didn't move from the seat for several minutes. Surprise held her there. She'd still been trying to cope with the long-buried warmth that had suffused her when Zac had taken her hand. When her mother had shown up, instinct had made her pull away. Zac's face had reflected anger—either at her haste in pulling away or at being interrupted. If there were other feelings there, she couldn't deal with them now.

Yes, she was infatuated with him, but that had to be it. She couldn't act on those yearnings and open herself up to that kind of pain again. And she dared not think he still liked her in that way, either, despite the way he'd looked at her as he'd held her hand.

Too many potential land mines lay ahead of them if they tried. She just wanted to solve this case then go back to her normal, practical, no-land-mines life.

Her predictable, lonely life.

Randi started to pay her bill but saw Zac had tossed down enough money for both of their meals. He'd paid—even after she might have dismissed genuine feelings on his part. It seemed the tables had turned and now she was the one owing him an apology.

She returned to her hotel room, flopped on the bed and stared at the ceiling. Thor came over, laid his head on the edge of the bed and stared at her, almost as if asking her to tell him her problems.

"You wouldn't understand, boy. I'm not sure I do." Randi rolled onto her side and saw the blinking message light on the phone. Her pulse leaped at the thought it might be Zac. She closed her eyes. She had to get the man out of her head—couldn't allow her fantasy to become reality. Even if she found the arsonist and wrapped up the case, Zac Parker was a bad idea. They lived in different towns, had different lives. And did she really need one more thing to distance her from her family?

She reached for the phone and punched the message button.

A muffled voice she couldn't distinguish said, "Stop asking questions if you know what's good for you."

Chapter Seven

Randi dropped the phone receiver as if the man was going to reach through and grab her. Zac was right. The guy was serious. Was she getting close to finding out his identity? Is that why he'd made the call? But why didn't she feel close?

She picked up the phone and punched the button to listen to the message again. No matter how hard she tried, she couldn't identify his voice or hear any recognizable sounds in the background. When someone knocked on the door, she jumped and yelped. Her reaction put Thor on alert. He sprang to his feet and stood ready to defend.

Randi hung up the phone and walked softly to the door, motioning for Thor to remain quiet as well. When she peeked through the peephole, there stood Zac.

As she tried to calm her racing heart and hide her emotions, she opened the door.

"Are we back to square one?"

She gripped the edge of the door, the initial shock of the call wearing off.

"Not from my perspective."

"You sure about that? You don't exactly look thrilled to see me."

Randi let out a long sigh. "Just a frustrating day." She must have let her guard slip, because his expression changed from defensive to concerned.

"What is it?"

Randi reminded herself of her plan to apologize, to take advantage of any help Zac might offer, to try to let the past go. "Listen, I'm sorry about what happened at lunch. Mom startled me."

"And you didn't want anyone you knew to see us together." He shrugged. "No problem."

She let go of the door and crossed her arms. "If that was the case, why did I eat lunch with you in a public place?"

"As long as no one in your family sees."

"Don't go making a big deal out of this. Now, why are you here?"

He looked as if he might tell her to go take a leap into the Gulf. "I got some information from Emily. Are we going to discuss it out here or can I come in?"

Randi hesitated before letting Zac enter the room. Once inside, he leaned against the desk while she sat at the small table.

"I'm afraid it's not much. I have no idea if it'll help."

"What did she find out?"

"She talked to the guy who made the harassment charge, but he wasn't in a sharing kind of mood. She did more digging, though, and found a couple of people in the area who thought maybe he'd gotten a nice cash payment to drop the suit. He bought a new car and made improvements to his store about the time the lawsuit was dropped."

Randi huffed. "Doesn't surprise me. Oldham's slick."

"Emily also found evidence that Oldham declared bankruptcy six years ago when one of his other building projects got into a financial bind."

Randi grabbed her notebook, determined to focus on work rather than the phone call or even the fact that she and Zac were together in a small space with a bed. "Now that's a little more interesting, though I've turned up nothing that indicates he is having any financial problems now. Still, something to consider." She jotted down the new information then glanced at the blinking light on the phone.

"Are you expecting a call?"

She jerked her gaze back toward him. "What?"

"You keep looking at the phone as if you're expecting a call." He directed his attention toward the phone. "Looks like you already have a message."

"Yeah."

He walked over and sank onto the edge of the opposite bed she was using as extra workspace. "What is it? Your brothers already find out you had lunch with me and ream you?"

She shook her head. "No." Suddenly very tired of keeping everything to herself, she decided to share with him. "It seems our arsonist is still perturbed that I'm asking questions."

Zac looked at the phone, picked up the receiver and hit the message button. She watched his face tighten as he listened. His eyes met hers, and there was the same concern she'd seen a few minutes before and in the restaurant earlier in the day.

A comforting warmth stole over her, hinting she might have less resistance to Zac than she thought. With him in the room, listening to the same message, she felt…safer.

He hung up the phone. "You should move to a safer place, one with indoor corridors and on-site security."

"I doubt he's going to break in here."

"He's threatened you twice."

"He may be just trying to scare me." Try as she might, she couldn't quite convince even herself.

"And maybe it's a three-strikes-and-you're-out kind of thing. This is strike two. You better hope you find this guy before I do." The muscles in Zac's forearms stretched as he fisted his hands.

"Don't do anything stupid. Hurting someone else isn't the best way to prove you're an innocent and trustworthy guy."

"Doesn't really seem to matter that I'm innocent. People are pretty quick to assume otherwise."

"Still, best to stay far away from trouble."

"So what about your moving?" Zac gave her a look filled with as much determination as she knew her own usually held.

"I'll check on it. I'm on the government dime here, and hotels with interior corridors and security cost more money."

"I doubt the government wants you in someone's crosshairs."

"Being a bit overdramatic, aren't you?" The image made her shiver nonetheless.

"Am I? Who knows how far desperate people will go?"

"I said I'd check on it. And I'll be careful." She pointed at him. "You, too. If this person figures out we're working together, he could just as easily take aim at you."

"Not as long as he thinks he can keep the suspicions cast toward me. I'm his best hope for staying undiscovered."

Another knock sounded at the door.

"Jeez, it's Grand Central Station," she said.

Zac stood.

"I'll get it." Randi got out of the chair and walked toward the door. "Do you really think the guy will show up here now without giving me a chance to heed his latest warning?"

Zac halted, but he stood near her as she answered the door.

Jack stood outside, his captain's uniform on. "Hey, Randi. I'm glad I caught you." He spotted Zac behind her. "Oh, sorry. I didn't know you had company." His eyes narrowed.

Randi hid her frustration that unexpected visits were making her alliance with Zac impossible to keep secret. "It's okay. Come on in." Randi strolled back to her spot at the table.

Jack hesitated at first then stepped inside. "Zac," he said, at least acknowledging his former colleague.

"Jack. I was just leaving." He looked at Randi, the intensity in his expression so powerful she felt it deep in her center. "Call and let me know what you find out."

She knew he was talking about the move to a different hotel, but she could already hear Steve worrying about the extra cost. It wasn't that her boss didn't care about her. He was just getting heat from above about cutting expenses. "Okay."

Once he'd left, closing the door behind him, Jack looked at her with a million questions in his expression.

"Don't start. I've had about enough today."

"You've always been a smart girl, but do you think that's wise?" He motioned toward the door Zac had exited.

"Listen, I don't have anything concrete pointing to Zac as the arsonist. If he's guilty, he'll slip up eventually. They always do." Her own guilt tugged at her as she spoke. It felt wrong to talk about Zac like that just to make sure Jack didn't think her incompetent. She paused, hesitated as she never had before at sharing her thoughts with Jack. She exhaled. She had to trust someone who wasn't a potential suspect. "In fact, it's possible someone is trying to set him up to take the fall."

"Will said you thought so. That's why I'm here. I want to make sure Parker doesn't pull the wool over your eyes if he's guilty."

Randi pressed the heel of her hand against her forehead in frustration and shook her head. "Not you, too. Give me some credit. And I don't need you suddenly thinking I'm the little girl who needs to be protected. I have a family that does that plenty fine, thanks." At least they used to.

"I didn't say that. You know I always thought they were too hard on you after the fire. But you and Zac were a couple. That could cloud anyone's judgment."

Randi walked to the other side of the room, trying not to spit back that Jack would never suggest such a thing if she were a guy. "I don't want to talk about it. If Zac is behind this, I'll find the evidence and use it. I'm just saying there's the possibility he's being framed."

"Just be careful."

"I always am."

Jack sighed, like a father might when dealing with an adult child he thought was making a mistake. "Any more luck?"

"No, but our guy did feel it necessary to call me."

Jack's eyes widened, almost in buggy, cartoon fashion. Must be the effect of his eyeglass lenses. "What did he say?"

She pointed to the phone. "Listen for yourself."

Jack picked up the receiver and listened as Zac

had. "Damn," he said after he hung up. "You think they can analyze the message, filter out whatever he was talking through?"

"Probably. But the caseload is heavy this summer. I'd be a decade older by the time they got around to it. But I'll report it to the police like I did the other stuff, just in case."

Jack stared at the phone, concern in his expression. "Have you told your parents or brothers?"

"No, and I'm not going to. The last thing I need is for them to suddenly think they need to barge back into my life. Though if I disappeared, most of them wouldn't notice."

Jack sank onto the end of the bed. "That's not true."

"Don't sit there and tell me you haven't noticed it. If there was ever tension you could truly cut with a knife, it's at the Cooke house anytime I walk in the door."

"It wasn't your fault, Randi."

How she wanted to believe those words, ached for them to be true. "Yes, it was. We all know that, and yet…it still hurts, Jack. You don't know how many times I've wished I could go back and do things differently. I'd still have my family."

Jack looked down at his wrinkled, tanned hands marred here and there by burn scars he'd sustained when not wearing protective gloves, stubborn old coot. "I miss having your dad around the station. He used to come by and hang out, but he eventually stopped. I think it made him miss fighting fires more."

Jack and her father had been best friends for years, and she knew Jack was hurt by what had happened. But this wasn't what she needed to hear right now. She shifted and pushed the power button on her laptop. "I really need to get back to work."

"Sorry, of course." Jack stood, some of his joints cracking in the process. "Be careful. And call me if you need anything. I might be old, but I'm still pretty sharp."

"Okay. Thanks. I might move to a different hotel if I can get Steve to approve a little more money per night."

"You want me to call him?"

"Nah, I've got it."

When Jack left, Randi sank against the inside of the door. Trying to forget about Jack, her family, even Zac, she focused instead on Oldham. Was something fishy there or was he just a class-A jerk? Her two phone conversations with him since the fire weren't what she'd call cordial. More like him questioning her professional ability.

She went to the phone and called the office. After she told Steve what had happened, he approved the hotel change. So, she spent the next hour checking out of the Coral Inn and into a room on the top floor of the three-story Sea Breeze, the tallest building in town since the Horizon Vista had never opened its doors. The hotel also overlooked the Beach Bum.

Once she unpacked her luggage and set up her computer on the much nicer desk, she walked onto the balcony and inhaled a deep breath of salty air. She glanced to her right and noticed two men in what looked like a heated argument at the top of the steps that led from the parking lot down to the beach. She leaned forward over the railing. Her heart lurched when she recognized them.

Zac and Bud Oldham looked like they were about to rip off each other's heads and feed them to the nearest bull shark.

Randi skipped the elevator and raced down the stairwell to the first floor. When she ran out the side door, she saw Oldham grab Zac's upper arm as he tried to walk away.

"I'd advise you to let him go," she said as she raised her voice.

"What?" Oldham bellowed as he turned to her.

She strode closer to the men. "Let Mr. Parker go." She enunciated each word to make herself perfectly clear.

"And if I don't?"

"Well, if he doesn't punch your lights out, we'll see what the police have to say about the situation."

Oldham gave her a nasty, angry look but released Zac, who mercifully kept his cool. "Maybe that's a good idea. I saw him sneaking around what little is left of my building." He looked at Zac with unmasked hatred. "There's nothing left to burn. You saw to that the first time around. Or maybe you're covering your tracks."

"Making baseless accusations will not endear you to the community, Mr. Oldham, and from what I've found out you could use a little positive promo," Randi said.

"And it seems you need some help to do your job."

Zac made a move toward Oldham, but Randi halted him by putting up her hand.

"You're more than welcome to call my boss. But he'll tell you I'm very good at my job, and I don't accuse people of a crime until I have proof. I question them, yes, but no accusations."

"You the one who's been snooping around in Tampa? Feels like you're trying to pin something on me."

She placed her hands in her pockets and met Oldham's stare. "If you have nothing to hide, there shouldn't be a problem."

Oldham jabbed his index finger in her direction. "I told you before I didn't have anything to do with the fire. So stop wasting time and look somewhere else." Oldham's face reddened beneath the tan veneer. "I want the person responsible found and prosecuted to the fullest extent of the law."

"He or she will be, but I suggest you let the professionals handle the investigation. Otherwise, you make yourself look bad."

Oldham looked like he wanted to say more, but he merely sent another angry look in Zac's direction then stalked away.

"That's getting really damned old," Zac said, his voice full of his own contained anger.

"Steer clear of him." She pointed toward the burned building. "What were you doing over there, anyway?"

"I was questioning the guys doing the cleanup. A lot of them were on the construction crew."

Randi crossed her arms. "Find out anything?"

"Nothing more than we already know—Oldham's a bastard."

"Then try not to put yourself in his path again."

"Gladly." He looked over at her then back at the direction from which she'd come. "Did you come out of the hotel?"

"Yeah. I took your advice and moved." She almost laughed at the surprise on his face. "Hey, I'm not stupid. Looks like this could take a while, and the view from here is better anyway." She gave in to the urge to smile at him.

He smiled back. Shivers of pure sexual awareness shot across her skin and made her warm and cold at the same time.

"I've got to get back to work," she said.

"Me, too. Come by for a drink after you're done."

"Okay." She did her best not to reveal how anxious she was for that time to arrive.

She spent the afternoon doing more digging that yielded nothing more than maybes and mights. She hated circumstantial evidence. Too much room for error. After checking her e-mail, she closed her laptop and rested her head against her upturned palms. Why couldn't she catch a break on this case?

Deciding to rest her brain, she went downstairs to use the weights in the fitness room. If only the room had a punching bag, she'd really be able to take out her frustration. The workout didn't provide her with the answers she sought, though she did feel better afterward. On the way back through the lobby, she spotted a pale blue halter dress in the hotel shop window. On impulse, she went inside the Sand Dollar and checked the rack for her size. When she found it, she stared at the material, wondering what made her want to buy a new outfit, and such a feminine one.

Zac, that's what.

She should forget the dress and walk out of the shop empty-handed. Instead, she bought it, a pair of white sandals with a big white daisy on top of each shoe and a pair of silver spiral earrings. When she returned to her room, Thor looked up from where he was sitting on the balcony watching the beach-goers. She held up her purchases. "Look, I went shopping."

When was the last time she'd gone clothes shopping for the sole purpose of impressing a man? Randi closed her eyes as she remembered. Before her first date with Zac. She'd had the hots for Zac bad. He seemed to be the one area of her life where brain cells failed her. That scared and excited her at the same time.

She thought about Zac the man rather than Zac the investigative partner as she showered and changed into her new clothing. She put her hair up in its customary ponytail, but when she caught her reflection in the mirror she took it down and let her hair fall free. Did she dare leave it that way? She rarely did, so would it be a dead giveaway she was on the verge of flirting with Zac? Of showing she was still attracted to him?

Feeling daring and needing a bit of fun to lighten her frustration with this case and the hurt of being so near and yet so far from her family, she left her hair down and stared at herself in the mirror. The combination of her loose hair caressing her bare back, the new fabric rubbing against her skin and thoughts of Zac aroused her. Her cheeks reddened. She had to get a grip before she really embarrassed herself.

After fanning her flushed face, she headed toward the door. On the way, she flipped on the TV and found Animal Planet. "Enjoy the boob tube, boy. You've earned a night off, too."

When she reached the Beach Bum, it was crowded with people who'd spent their day on the beach or out fishing the stunning and fruitful waters of the Gulf. Zac was filling orders and laughing with customers, and her blood surged with a yearning she'd not had in a long time. She wanted Zac to laugh with her.

Her heart leaped at the expression on Zac's face when he saw her, as if he were seeing a mirage. Mouth partly open, eyes more focused, perhaps resisting the urge to blink to see if the image disappeared. The dress had been worth every penny. She walked up to the bar and slid onto a stool next to Adam, whom she'd not seen since she'd talked to him that day on the pier—when he'd flirted outrageously with her.

Adam whistled. "Be still my heart. If you're here to arrest me, I'll go willingly."

Randi laughed. "You either get no girls with these crazy lines or you get lots of them. I can't decide."

Adam leaned toward her and waggled his eyebrows. "Did it work with you?"

"Sorry. I'm just here for a drink."

Adam glanced at Zac. "Uh-huh. So, Zac, doesn't the lady clean up well?"

Zac pulled two beers from the cooler and handed them to one of the waitresses. "Yeah, you look nice." Randi caught his gaze before he turned around and started fixing a mixed drink.

Adam chuckled beside her. "Man, you would make a terrible poker player. You can't hide your thoughts worth crap." He looked over at Randi and winked. "Pardon me while I work the crowd and see if any young lady would like to go for a stroll on the beach."

Randi couldn't help giving him a wide smile. He was a ladies' man, but he was funny and friendly.

When Adam vacated his spot, Zac turned around. "You do look nice. What's the occasion?"

She shrugged. "No occasion. Just felt like a break. I'm tired of beating my head against the wall. I'm fairly certain I have no skin left on my forehead. For a case that has so many people who hated the victim, I'm coming up with squat."

"Nothing more on Oldham?"

She shook her head. "I spent hours digging, and while he is undoubtedly a jerk and a bully, I can't find any evidence that says he would have had a reason to start this fire."

Adam returned, a lovely, tall brunette in tow. They circled around behind the bar.

Zac stepped back and gave his friend a questioning look. "What are you doing?"

"Brooke here is a licensed bartender. She's going to fill in for you, and I'm going to help."

"What are you talking about? Did you start drinking before you got here?"

Adam clapped Zac on the back. "You, my friend, need a night off. You never take time off."

Zac grabbed three beers for a customer but kept his attention on Adam. "You've lost your mind."

"No, but you have if you don't take this lovely lady to dinner," he said, indicating Randi.

"Really, it's okay. I'm just here for a drink and to unwind," Randi said, though she was secretly thrilled at the thought of actually going to dinner with Zac. Like she'd been a few years ago when she'd finally relented to his persistent flirting and gone out with him the first time.

"I hear you can get a drink and unwind at many of our fine restaurants in town," Adam said, undeterred.

"Adam—" Zac began.

"Dude, just go." Adam crossed his arms, emphasizing how big they were. "I am a champion at making scenes, and I don't think you want that."

Zac looked at Randi, and all she could do was offer a smile and a shrug. "Fine. If you want to work all night, be my guest."

Randi tried not to think of dinner with Zac as a date. It was only dinner, a break from work for both of them.

When he rounded the bar and reached her side, he

looked as if he might offer his arm but then changed his mind. "Well, where to?"

Randi tried not to focus on how much she'd wanted to take his arm. "Doesn't matter."

He looked down at his jeans and Beach Bum T-shirt. "I'm not really dressed for dinner. I could go home and change."

"No need. We could get takeout and find a picnic table."

Zac nodded. "Sounds good to me."

They walked to the parking lot. "Mind if I drive?" he asked.

She shoved aside her need to be in control of every situation. "No."

They grabbed sandwiches and chips from a deli then Zac drove out to the near edge of the National Seashore.

"No picnic tables, but I have a couple of lawn chairs in the back," he said. "And you don't have to worry who'll see you."

Randi looked over at him, an unexpected feeling of shame washing over her. "Zac—"

"It's okay, really." He sounded genuine, which alleviated some of her regret at having treated him like a hot potato when her mom had surprised them at the restaurant.

She wanted to explain to him, but she was embarrassed by her reasoning. How pathetic was it that she hoped if she did everything just right, her family would love her again? "I'm not ashamed to be seen with you. It's just…"

"You don't have to explain. Why give them more ammo, right?"

She looked at him, amazed by his understanding. "Thanks."

"Be careful. Keep apologizing to me and you're

going to ruin your reputation as a tough cookie." He glanced over at her with a crooked smile that made her want to lean across and kiss him.

"Well, we can't have that." She grabbed the door handle. "I'll take the food. You get the chairs," she said, then opened the passenger-side door.

He caught up with her, a chair in each hand, as she crossed the dunes. He followed wordlessly as she walked down to the edge of the beach in her bare feet, her new shoes dangling from her right hand, so they could sit next to the incoming tide.

As they ate, Randi caught Zac watching her lips as she licked her fingers. Or was she imagining things? The jittery feeling that came over her made her feel like a lovesick teenager. They talked about ships on the horizon, how Adam was never without a date and Thor's penchant for watching Animal Planet.

"How long have you had him?" Zac asked.

"Little over two years. The big lug is my best friend. And very good at his job."

"I'm surprised he's not with you now."

"Even best friends need time apart. I've been dragging him all over since I've been here. He's usually a good judge of people as well as accelerants."

"So, who has he not liked?"

"Oldham. And a guy on the beach the other morning who was hooting catcalls at me when I was jogging."

"I don't think I like that guy, either."

To hide the effect his words had on her pulse, she resorted to teasing. She smiled and brought her clasped hands to her chest. With a theatrical voice, she closed her eyes and said, "Oh, my knights in shining armor. Whatever would I do without you?"

"Not this," Zac whispered close to her, and then his lips touched hers.

She jumped and opened her eyes wide.

Zac pulled back and looked at her. "Tell me to stop."

She couldn't. All the reasons identifying this as a bad idea zipped through her brain. She ignored them and leaned into him, accepted his kiss with an explosion of longing that would have scared her if she'd stopped to think.

Slowly, Zac pulled away. Randi's heartbeat thundered in her ears. Louder even than the waves now rushing over their feet.

"Guess we should move before we're carried out to sea," he said, his breath cooling the wetness on her lips.

"Yeah." She didn't sound as if she wanted to move at all, but when Zac stood and lifted his chair, she did the same. When she set hers down several feet farther up the beach, Zac pulled her into his arms.

"This has nothing to do with when we were together before. And this has nothing to do with the case."

How could simply being held in a man's arms feel so good, so…perfect? She looked up at him. "Why are you doing this?"

"Because I like it." And then he kissed her again, longer and deeper this time, with her pulled close to the length of his hard body. The sea breeze seemed to have a sense for matchmaking, pushing them together. Warmth wholly unrelated to the season stole over her skin.

She let go of some final bit of control and kissed him back with all the sexual yearning trapped inside her, trying to claw its way out. Her arms snaked around his neck, her fingers into the soft texture of his hair. Her scalp tingled when he ran his fingers through the long strands of her loose hair. The way he pressed against her caused the fabric of her dress to rub across her breasts, bringing back the arousal she'd felt in the hotel earlier. She moaned into his warm mouth.

Zac eventually ended the kiss but kept gifting her with soft kisses on her cheeks, her forehead, her ears. The scary thought that she could fall for him again, hard, occurred to her. She pulled back and looked at him. She should step away, arm herself with distance, but he felt too good. The overwhelming desire to believe they could start over battered against her like an invading army attacking the castle gate.

He rubbed the backs of his fingers along her cheek. "Stop thinking. Just go with it." He lowered his mouth close to hers again and kissed her with such tenderness she nearly wept. Too late, she realized she was already falling for Zac Parker all over again.

A little voice at the back of her mind whispered that she was doing it again, letting instinct take over. And look what had happened the last time she'd done that. She'd nearly killed her father.

But heaven help her, she couldn't stop. She prayed she was right this time, that going with her instinct wasn't a huge mistake.

Chapter Eight

Suddenly, Zac jerked away, causing Randi to gasp and stumble. What had she done to make him stop? A flash of movement and the sickening sound of a punch against bone and flesh made her gasp. Zac stumbled backward. Will grabbed Zac's arm to pull him back to his feet so he could hit him again.

Randi leaped at him and screamed, "Stop it! Stop!"

Will Cooke in a rage was roughly equivalent to a full-grown grizzly in a really bad mood. He outweighed her by seventy pounds and was deaf to her pleas. He struck Zac again, but Zac threw a punch of his own and made contact with Will's jaw.

"Hold him!" Will yelled.

Movement out of the corner of Randi's eye proved to be Karl.

"Don't you dare!" she screamed at her other brother. He halted, looking between her and the continuing fight. "Stop them," she begged, but he didn't take a step.

Anger burning, Randi grabbed one of the lawn chairs, folded it and hit her oldest brother with it. He managed to knock the chair away but stepped back from Zac long enough for her to move between them.

Both of them tried to maneuver past her to get at the other again, but she pushed against their chests. When Will attempted to set her aside, she'd had enough. She slapped him as hard as she could. The force of the blow made her palm burn.

Will staggered then looked at her as if he couldn't believe she'd dare hit him.

Randi's breathing came in heavy gasps, and she heard similar sounds from Zac behind her. "Stop it," she hissed at Will, "or I swear I'll punch you next time."

Will massaged his jaw. "What's wrong with you?"

Randi flung her arms out in exasperation. "Me? You're the one flying out of nowhere attacking people."

He shook his head. "Don't you see? God, Randi, you used to be so smart. What happened to you?"

"Watch your mouth, Cooke," Zac said through clenched teeth.

Randi's eyes filled with tears. How had she so totally lost her brother to the spiteful man he'd become? "Let me guess. You think Zac is kissing me so I can't think and see he's a crafty arsonist right under my nose? That about right?"

"Something like that," he spit back at her. He gave Zac a hard stare. "Did he tell you the things he said about our family? That we were a disgrace to our uniforms? That someday we'd get our due? Is this our due, Parker? Seducing our sister?"

Zac tried to get past her again, but she pushed against him, causing him to lose his footing in the loose sand and halting his progress.

"That's low, even for you," Will continued.

"Shut up," Randi said, low and threatening.

Will stared at her like he couldn't fathom who she

was, like she couldn't claim two IQ points. "I can't believe you're not suspicious. He's been charged with arson before. And I don't care that he was cleared. It was just fishy the way that woman changed her story. Even Jack said so."

"Mom doesn't think so."

That revelation stopped Will for a moment, but then he shook his head. "Mom's too trusting."

She expelled a mirthless laugh. "I'd like to see you say that to her face."

Will growled in frustration. "Randi, can't you see he's using you?"

Zac uttered a dangerous, feral growl and took a step behind her.

"I guess it didn't occur to you that maybe somebody gives a damn about me." She ignored the burning in her eyes.

"I give a damn! Why else would I be out here?"

She shook her head with a sadness so deep it threatened to crush her soul. "I don't know, Will. Maybe you like being in control, maybe you're afraid I'll be even more of an embarrassment to the family, maybe you like reminding me that I made a mistake and can't be trusted to think on my own anymore." She jabbed her right index finger in the air. "One mistake, Will! One!"

"And it was a damn big one!"

Randi swiped at a stupid tear that chose that moment to slip free of her eye. Zac placed his hands on her shoulders for support, but he thankfully let her fight this battle because it was hers to fight. "Don't you think I know that? I think about it every day. I have nightmares about it. If I could go back and change it, I would. But

I can't, and I've paid for it. I lost the most important thing in my life—my family."

They stared at each other for a few painful, hushed seconds in which the entire world seemed to have forgotten how to breathe. She saw disappointment in his eyes and felt as if her insides were being shredded with a thousand knives. Not able to stand it anymore, she turned to leave.

"Randi—"

"Leave me alone, Will. That shouldn't be too hard. You've had three years of practice."

ZAC WATCHED as Randi stalked away, her bare feet kicking up sand as she left one brother behind and ignored the other when she passed him. Sympathy for her and anger at her brothers welled up inside him. He started after Randi, but Will caught his arm.

"Don't you dare hurt her."

Zac wrenched himself free and fought the urge to beat the living hell out of Will. "I hadn't planned on it. Looks like you've got that under control yourself."

Neither Will nor Karl tried to stop him again as he hurried down the beach.

"Randi."

"Go away."

He caught her and, despite her initial efforts to get away from him, he succeeded in pulling her into his arms, guiding her head against his chest. She resisted for several moments before her body relaxed and she allowed him to hold her.

Odd how even the strongest of women could feel fragile at times. He pulled her closer, loving the feel of her next to him but hating the reason she needed comforting. She shook as her tears dampened the front of his T-shirt. He lifted a hand and stroked her hair. "Shh. It's okay."

"No, it's not. It's never going to be okay."

Damn Will Cooke to hell for tearing his sister apart like this. Families were supposed to be supportive and love one another. Will hadn't done either. Zac thought of his own father, fueling his anger further. Why did families have to hurt each other so much?

Zac looked down the beach to where Will and Karl stood watching them. Hatred burned in Will's gaze, and Zac wondered why that hatred was so strong.

Karl said something to his brother and headed for the parking lot. Will stared several seconds more before following.

Only when they disappeared over the dunes did Zac drop a kiss onto the top of Randi's silky hair. He didn't force her to talk, just held her and let her know without words that he wasn't going anywhere, that he would be there to hold her when she needed it.

He didn't want to leave her side. She was a tough woman who'd held her own in a man's world, but that didn't make him want to protect her any less. Though he couldn't say that out loud. She'd made it abundantly clear she didn't like being coddled, and he didn't blame her. Not if "protection" resulted in the actions her brother had taken minutes before.

"Are you ready to leave?" he asked.

She shook her head. "I'd rather walk on the beach for a while. You can go. I'll walk back to the hotel."

Zac leaned back and looked into her eyes. "Do you really think I'd do that after what just happened? After everything that's happened lately?"

For the first time since he'd met her, Randi looked unsure. She lifted her fingertips and ran them gently along his throbbing jaw. "I'm sorry."

"It's not your fault. Will just acts before he thinks."

"It's a family trait." Her voice was so full of sadness it broke his heart.

Zac looked toward the water then back at her. "What he said was true, what I said about your family. It wasn't just that they didn't stand behind me. Will nearly shoved me out of the department, said they had a long reputation of integrity and didn't need anyone ruining that. I never hated someone so much."

Fresh tears pooled in Randi's eyes. "I don't know everything that happened between the two of you back when you were charged, but this—" she said as she pointed to where Will had punched him "—has way more to do with me than you."

"Does he go around punching every guy you kiss?"

"Not that there are that many, but no. Of course, he doesn't get the chance." She sighed, then started walking down the beach into the growing darkness.

Zac's hand curled around hers as if it were the most natural thing he'd ever done, as if time and hurtful words had never passed between them. She didn't pull away, which gave him hope for them. They walked for probably two full minutes before Randi spoke again.

She let go of his hand and hugged herself. "What's so painful is that Will has good reason to be angry at me. I try so hard to make good, sound decisions now because of the huge mistake I made during that fire." She stopped and looked out at the dark waves.

Zac stared toward the Gulf, too, instinct telling him she didn't want touches or eye contact as she delved into the past. She needed to voice these sorrows even though he'd seen them firsthand.

"I grew up a tomboy, and I adored my brothers. When they all became firefighters like my dad and grandpa, it seemed logical that I would, too. They had never minded me riding dirt bikes, going deep-sea fishing, playing baseball, running track. But when I said I was going to become a firefighter, they balked. Suddenly, they saw me as a girl, fragile, someone to be excluded from their world. And it ticked me off." She let out a slow sigh.

"I went to college, even worked as a kindergarten teacher for a while, believe it or not. But just to show them, I trained to be a firefighter, too. I did really well in all the training. When I applied for the job here, I badgered Dad until he hired me. As Will pointed out, the Cookes have a long history with the department, and Dad couldn't say I didn't know my stuff. And…I was pretty militant about my ability and how I didn't want to be treated differently. I think Dad finally caved because he wanted me to be here where he and my brothers could watch out for me rather than at another department where they couldn't."

For several seconds, she watched the waves. Zac wondered if she was already regretting sharing more of her past with him tonight than she had the entire two months they'd dated.

"But even after I joined the department, they all tried to keep me out of dangerous situations. It took forever for them to even let me near a fire. I drove the truck, did crowd control, school fire safety programs. All those things are important, but that they didn't trust me to hold my own grated on my last nerve."

She picked up a piece of a seashell and pitched it into the water. The plop was masked by the sound of the incoming waves.

"I'd been there six months before I went into a fire. We had a big barn fire out in the county, and they needed every hand. I did well, but they still insisted it was too dangerous for me to do on a regular basis. I went in on several more fires when they didn't have a choice, and I always held my own. I never complained about how much the gear weighed, how I stank after a fire, nothing. Even after you joined the department, they were still playing that 'protect the baby sister' game." She paused again, stared into the waves as if they formed a screen on which her life's history played. He sensed what was next.

"And then we had that fire out on Sandbar Lane," she said, her voice lowering with sorrow and repressed tears. "It was burning so hot and fast. You remember how we worked like crazy to get it under control." The look on her face, the distance of her voice—she was back there, reliving that horrible day.

If he thought about it, he, too, could still feel the heat and ferocity of those flames, wind-whipped and hungry, consuming the vacation rental. He remembered the combination of defeat and relief he'd felt when Randi's father had issued the order to get out before the roof caved in. And the horror of what happened once they got outside. The woman looking at the house and screaming for her little girl—and Randi heading back into the flames against orders.

Zac's gut twisted when he thought of watching her disappear into that monster. He'd fought hard to get free of Jack, Karl and Josh so he could go after her, to no avail.

"I didn't consider my own safety or anyone else's but that child's. The place was on the verge of collapsing when I ran back in, but I didn't care." She shuddered. "I can still hear the woman's cries, the roar of the fire…and Will yelling at me to come back. I have nightmares about the sound the roof made as it began to cave in, about how when I turned to leave, I saw that beam fall and hit Dad across his back." Her voice caught, but she cleared it and went on. "I still don't know how I moved it. It weighed more than I did and was on fire, but I somehow managed to shove it off him and started dragging Dad out. And then Will appeared in the smoke and took him."

Zac had never felt such relief as when he'd seen Eric pull Randi out just before the roof gave way. And then anger at her for scaring him—all of them—like that.

"The first thing I saw when I got out was the woman hugging her daughter. It hit me she'd been outside the entire time, that my foolish rescue attempt had been for nothing." Her voice cracked as it faded away. "When I found out Dad knew the girl was outside before I rushed back in, I wanted to die."

Zac glanced in her direction. The ambient light from the stars showed the tears rolling silently down her cheeks. He didn't pull her into his arms as he wanted to, rather took her hand in his. She squeezed it in what felt like a gesture of gratitude.

"Will blamed me for that beam crushing Dad's spine, and rightly so. I'd gone with my gut instead of my training. And my dad paid the price."

That last part explained so much about Randi and how she conducted her investigations. Facts—cold, hard, irrefutable facts—that's all she would rely on anymore.

She looked over at him. "That's why you scare me."

"Me?"

"You've got me wanting to go with my gut again, and there's nothing that frightens me more."

Zac turned toward her and stared into her eyes, their beautiful blue not visible in the dim light. "I'm doing everything I can to prove it wasn't me and find the person who really set the fire. To show you that you're right to believe in me despite what happened before."

"I know."

The deep pain of losing the closeness she'd once shared with her family still clouded her expression.

"I know nothing I can say will likely change the way you feel about what happened, but people make mistakes. And sometimes they have consequences for other people." He squeezed her hand and gave it a gentle shake. "But what good does it do to live the rest of your life not forgiving yourself? You can't go back and change what happened, but how you live now is totally up to you."

"It's not that simple."

"Never said it was. It'll be damned hard if Will's reaction tonight is any indication. But he was right about one thing."

"What?"

"If he didn't care about you under all that anger, he wouldn't have given a rat's ass who you were kissing." To give Will Cooke any credit ate at him, but this was about Randi's feelings, not his.

She stood silent, as if soaking in what he'd said and mulling the truth of his words.

"Randi, you fought hard to be a firefighter, to be where you are now, to be successful in all the cases you've worked. Maybe it's time to fight to get your family back."

"I've tried," she said, sounding bone-deep tired.

"Then try again. You don't give up on your cases. Don't give up on this."

She shook her head. "But—"

"No buts. This isn't just for you. I'll bet other members of your family want this, too, but no one wants to take the first step. It's easier to keep going along the way you have been since the accident than to bring up all that old blame and pain."

Randi tilted her head and pinned him with a searching look. "You sure you trained to be a firefighter and not a psychologist?"

He laughed. "Bartending will do that to a guy."

"Do people really tell you all their problems?"

"You wouldn't believe."

She smiled then, and his heart lifted that he'd been able to put the smile on her face. And he hoped he hadn't given her bad advice. He hoped her family cooperated.

Randi started walking down the beach, back toward the lawn chairs. "Tell me what happened between you and my brothers."

"You know most of it."

"Did they automatically assume you were guilty?"

Despite all the anger he'd harbored against her family, he had to look at the situation dispassionately now. Tonight was the night for brutal honesty.

"At first, I think they wanted to believe me. But the 'witness' testimony was damaging and the so-called evidence built up quickly. Their support faded just as fast. They didn't want to be associated with a firefighter who could have betrayed them and his career. And they…"

"What?"

"They still had your dad's accident fresh on their minds then, and they weren't inclined to take it easy on a potential arsonist."

She understood that. The fact that an arsonist was responsible for the fire that had changed the lives of her and her family was one of the main reasons she'd become an arson investigator.

"But what about the police?"

"I tried to tell the cops that Trina wasn't what you'd call stable, but they wouldn't listen. Your family's word carries a lot of weight around here. And Trina was quite the actress, too. Fitting she moved to California after she served her sentence." Zac let out a long sigh. "At the time, I felt I'd been sacrificed to the wolves. Still do."

"But you didn't find another firefighter position."

"The whole thing made me want to walk away. Plus, who would hire a firefighter who's been accused of arson?"

Something flickered at the back of Randi's brain, but she was too tired and wrung out to catch it before it flitted away.

"Why did you stay in Horizon Beach?"

"I liked it. That's why I moved here in the first place. I'd bought a house. I'd bartended some in Tallahassee when I lived there, so I thought I'd give that a whirl. It seemed a fairly carefree way to make a living. Still work, but I wasn't going to be running into burning buildings. Or watching people I cared about risking their lives." He thought back to how angry he'd been. "Plus, I wasn't real up on serving the greater good of society at that point. It didn't matter how many years I'd been a firefighter or how good I was at my job. One accusation erased all that."

Randi stopped and looked toward the glow of Horizon Beach in the distance. "Fate just sucks sometimes, doesn't it?"

He smiled. "Yeah, that about sums it up." He turned her to face him, trying not to crowd but letting her know he liked holding her. "I'm glad I stayed even if I did have to see your brothers' mugs fairly often."

"Why?"

"If I'd left, I would never have seen you again."

A small smile eased some of the sadness in her eyes. "I'm sure you wished you hadn't that first day."

"Not the best reunion ever." He kissed her forehead. "But even then, I thought you were still the most beautiful woman I'd ever seen. Definitely the most beautiful person to ever accuse me of a crime."

She pulled back. "I didn't accuse you. I was asking—"

He stifled her protest with a kiss, soft at first but then deepening when she relaxed against him. How good she tasted, how soft she felt in his arms.

Randi leaned back slightly, inhaled, looked up at him. "I'm surprised you can kiss after the way Will decked you."

"Kissing makes it better." He waggled his eyebrows, making her laugh. After kissing her until he thought he would explode from wanting her, he pulled away but held her hand as he guided her toward the parking area.

She didn't resist, didn't question, simply followed.

They retrieved the chairs and her sandals and made their way wordlessly over the dunes. Zac barely registered the crash of the waves or the easy way the vegetation clinging to the dunes swayed in the breeze. What he heard above all else was the surging of his pulse as he thought about taking Randi back to her room, laying her across the bed with her long hair loose, and making love to her to the rhythm of the ocean.

By the time they reached his Jeep, he had to taste her again. He dropped his chair on the pavement and leaned her against the side of the vehicle. He tangled his hands in her silky hair then ran them down the cool skin of her exposed back as he kissed her deeply and thoroughly.

"Did you wear that dress to drive me crazy?" he asked against her lips.

Her mouth curved up into a smile. "No. I thought it was pretty. But driving you crazy is a nice extra benefit."

"You were right about it being pretty." Had he ever kissed a woman so much in one night? Even her? Randi Cooke was quickly wiping the thought of other women from his memory. "What's your name?"

She pulled back and looked at him as if he'd lost his mind.

Zac traced her eyebrows with his index finger. "I doubt Randi is your full name. Sounds like the name a tomboy gives herself. But you sure don't look or feel like a tomboy now."

"You know my name."

"No, I don't. You never told me, and I never heard anyone call you anything but Randi."

After a pause in which she seemed to be considering keeping her real name a mystery, she said, "Miranda. Miranda Leann. Though it sounds odd to me now. No one calls me that."

He leaned close to her ear. "When you look this sexy, you need the sexy name…Miranda."

Shivers ran over Randi's skin at the sexy growl of her name on Zac's lips. A normal name she rarely used sounded erotic coming from him. But then, that could be because she was on the verge of dragging him off to a soft dune and making love to him beneath the stars. Her nerve endings popped like firecrackers, and her skin tingled with the need to be even closer to Zac.

When was the last time she'd wanted to have sex this much? That first time with Zac? Maybe it wasn't the smartest move in the world, but she didn't care. After the way he'd listened to her tonight, the way he'd held her without making her feel like a helpless woman, she couldn't believe it would be a mistake. She was taking Zac Parker into her life again and seeing where it led.

They managed to pull their heated bodies apart long enough to get into the Jeep. Zac kissed her again then groaned and started the engine.

Randi's heart wouldn't behave as Zac drove them back toward town. She knew where they were heading and why, and it took what little sense she had left not to tackle him while he was driving. When he nearly two-wheeled it into the hotel parking lot, she didn't wait for him to come around to her side. She jumped out and met him on his.

He pulled her to him and kissed her again. Dear Lord, he was turning her into a mindless puddle of goo.

"If this isn't what you want, you'd better tell me to take a hike now," he said.

Randi looked up at the star-sprinkled sky. "It's too late to be hiking."

He took her answer as she'd intended and led her toward the side entrance to the hotel. What had been an upsetting evening was definitely looking up. The sounds of laughter from the beach drew her attention.

"Sounds like Adam has everything under control."

"Good, because I'm not going back to work tonight." He stopped and pulled her against him again. "I'm going to make love to you with the balcony door open so we can hear the waves."

Randi's skin heated so much it was a good thing she wasn't near any combustibles.

As they wove through the lines of parked cars, she caught sight of hers. Something white was stuck underneath the driver's-side windshield wiper. Probably an ad telling her what a good deal one of the tourist shops had on flip-flops and genuine sand dollars. When they got closer, however, she realized it wasn't an ad at all. Her name stood out in big block letters on the front of a plain, letter-size envelope. She stopped.

"Don't have second thoughts now," Zac said in a pained voice.

Randi didn't respond, rather let Zac's hand go and went to retrieve the envelope. Before opening it, she looked at both sides but didn't see anything to indicate who'd left it. A cold, sinking feeling settled in her chest as she slid her finger underneath the flap and opened the envelope.

Zac stepped up beside her, a comforting presence.

Randi pulled out a sheet of paper and unfolded it. What looked like a Polaroid photo dropped onto the hood of the car. She left it as she read the short note written in the same blocky letters.

"I told you to stop."

She turned the photo face up. The blood drained from her head, and she had to put her hand out against the car to keep from falling. The photo was of a black Lab. A very dead black Lab.

Chapter Nine

Randi raced to the top floor of the hotel. Thor had to be safe, he had to be. Throughout the loneliest years of her life, he'd been there, loving her unconditionally. When she reached the room, Zac right behind her, she fumbled and dropped the key card. "Damn it!"

Tears pooled in her eyes as she picked it up and slid it through the card reader. She threw the door open and saw Thor, standing there in the middle of the room waiting to greet her. A sob poured from her as she dropped the note and picture and fell to her knees in front of him. When she wrapped her arms around him and hugged him to her, he whined in protest. Still, she didn't let him go until she'd convinced herself he was whole and unharmed.

But some other dog wasn't. Had the arsonist killed a poor animal just to scare her? Her blood chilled at the thought.

As Randi tried to calm herself, she became aware that Zac was on the phone. She focused on his words and realized he was calling the police. This time, she was thankful someone else was there to step in and take over.

Thor tired of her hugs and examinations and pulled away to resume his favorite spot on the balcony. Zac helped her to her feet and into his arms. "The police will be here soon."

He was right—two officers showed up within five minutes.

"Hi, Randi." Oscar Benjamin, a middle-aged officer she'd known during her days with the fire department, walked past Zac into the room.

"Oscar," she said, her voice a bit shaky.

"I heard you got quite a scare."

She handed him the note and photo. "I thought it was my dog."

Oscar looked over to where Thor now sat next to the TV, observing the extra activity. "He wasn't with you when you found the note?"

"No. He was here in the room."

Oscar looked at the picture and grimaced. "Then this guy either knew that and wanted you to think he'd killed your dog, or he wasn't aware you two weren't together and he just meant it as a warning."

"I don't really care what he meant. It's still cruel. He killed an animal for no reason." Randi heard her words, but they sounded so distant, as though she was in shock. Just like that, she could have lost Thor. Would the next threat be against her family? She'd underestimated how dangerous the arsonist was.

"He's definitely escalated the violence. When you continue your investigation, you need to be extra cautious. Carry protection or, I'd suggest, get some backup," Oscar said.

"And where were you when all this happened?" asked the other patrolman, a younger man. But by the narrow-eyed look of suspicion on his face, he was still enough of a veteran to remember Zac's last brush with the law.

"He was with me," Randi said. "He had nothing to do with it."

"Are you—?"

"Give it a rest, Mike," Oscar said. "He was cleared."

Randi wasn't sure if Oscar was talking about tonight or two years ago, but she was surprised by the support regardless. She glanced at Zac. Will's words came back to her despite her anger toward him.

He's lying to you.

No, she wasn't going to resort to crazy conspiracy theories. No doubt that was exactly what the arsonist wanted. She sank onto the bed and rubbed her eyes, trying to erase any doubts.

During the next several minutes, Randi answered all the typical questions: Where had she been and for how long? Did she have any clue who might have done this? Had she seen anything else suspicious?

"You might want to move to another location," Oscar said when he flipped his notebook shut.

"I've already moved hotels once. That doesn't seem to be a deterrent." Which meant the person knew her movements. Who knew? Zac—he'd been with her. Jack—about as likely to threaten her as her own father. Her family—though they didn't know why she'd moved. Adam and Suz—but they were busy at the bar.

"Is there…somewhere else you could stay?" Oscar asked. He evidently knew all about the rift in her family. She doubted there were many residents of Horizon Beach who didn't. Randi looked Oscar in the eye to let him know she understood what he was suggesting. "No, I'll stay here."

Oscar nodded, perhaps not agreeing but recognizing her right to make her own decision. "We'll check with the staff and look at the surveillance video."

"If he didn't hide the camera again," Zac said.

"This one's too high up unless he was carrying a ladder with him," Oscar said. "Someone would have noticed."

When the two officers left, Randi rose and walked out onto the balcony. Thor followed and plopped down in his favorite people-watching spot.

"Whoever sent the note knows how much Thor means to you," Zac said from where he stood in the doorway behind her. "And it's not just because he's your partner."

Thor looked up at the sound of his name. Zac stepped onto the balcony and scratched him between the ears. Thor ate it up, oblivious to the human drama going on around him.

"It's someone I know."

"At least someone who's been watching you closely."

Her skin chilled more than the breeze off the water warranted. As if this night couldn't get any worse.

RANDI OPENED her eyes and blinked, disoriented. A few seconds passed before she realized she'd fallen asleep. She lay on top of the comforter, still in the halter dress she'd worn the night before. But there was a blanket draped over her. Where…?

She glanced over and saw Zac asleep in one of the room's chairs. His head leaned at an angle sure to cause a neck ache, and his long legs stretched out in front of him. She looked toward the partially open sliding-glass door where Thor was spread out snoring. Pink light heralded the start of another day.

She returned her focus to Zac. He'd spent the night. Her heart swelled, and she feared it was the beginnings of love. But she couldn't afford to love someone else. Didn't she have enough people in her life she had loved and lost?

Not ready to face the day and the ugliness of the note and photo, Randi laid her head on her pillow and watched the rise and fall of Zac's chest. Remembered the way he'd kissed her, listened to her, held her, had almost made love to her. She wanted him like no man she'd ever met. But in the light of day, she wondered again if it was a mistake. Was she even capable of loving without doubts anymore? Shouldn't she just stick with work and leave fancies of falling in love for younger, less damaged women?

Zac's jaw was bruised this morning, and she hated that her brother had been the one to mar such a handsome face. She resisted the urge to slip from the bed and kiss his cheek because, as soon as she did and he woke, the reality of a new day would hit. No more magical kisses beneath the stars. She'd have to figure out who was so evil that not only would he burn down a building for no obvious gain but also butcher an innocent dog just to scare her. She stared at the ceiling.

No obvious gain. Maybe that was it. The idea that the fire had nothing to do with revenge or money hit her with more force than it had a few days before when she'd first considered it might be a random act. She still hoped to identify a real "reason" behind the fire, but perhaps the arsonist was simply setting fires because he got a thrill out of it. And he didn't take kindly to someone possibly ending his fun. Was this the only fire he'd set? Or were there others? She'd have to check with Jack or Eric, see if they had any more unsolved fires in the area, ones for which she wouldn't have been called in. She'd already read over the information about fires where the state had been assigned the cases.

Zac grunted. Randi turned to find him awake with a pinched look on his face.

"Maybe a hot shower will get rid of the kinks," she said.

He rolled his neck and winced. "I think I need a full-body massage."

Randi swallowed while she tried to focus on anything but running her hands all over Zac's naked body. "Sorry I fell asleep. You didn't have to stay."

"I wasn't going anywhere. As hard as the chair is, at least I slept. I wouldn't have if I'd gone home and left you here alone." He massaged the muscles in his neck.

"I wouldn't have been alone."

He pinned her with a serious look. "The guy has proved a dog is no match for him."

The sickening image from the photo flashed in her mind and nearly made her gag. "I'd like to think he wouldn't be so careless as to come into the hotel. So far he's stayed outside. Plus, he'd already made his move for the evening."

"Maybe, but I wouldn't have slept anyway." Zac stood and stretched, making his bones crack audibly.

Randi got up as well and smoothed her messy hair. "You could have slept on the bed."

Zac stared at her, a bit of the heat from the night before back in his eyes. "That wouldn't have been a good idea."

"Why not?"

"Because you'd had a scare, and it wasn't the right time for doing what I would have wanted to do."

"You could have just…" She let her words fade away, ones that would reveal how much she was beginning to care for him.

He took the few steps it required for him to reach her. "Just what?"

She looked up at him. "…held me."

Zac pulled her to him now, and she sank against his strength and warmth. Why did this feel so right? So safe? Like life before Zac had been woefully incomplete?

He kissed the top of her head. "I think I'll take that shower now."

Randi blushed when she considered he might be taking a cold one instead.

"Don't suppose you'd want to join me?" he asked, a teasing smile curving his lips.

Her body went up in flames. "I'll take a rain check."

He kissed her on the forehead and headed toward the bathroom. "Don't go anywhere until I get out."

She experienced a knee-jerk reaction against the command, but he'd likely been scared by the photo the night before as well and worried for her. She needed to cut him a little slack.

While she brushed her teeth at the sink outside the bathroom, the phone rang. Her heart stuttered as she spun to look at it. She stared at the phone as it rang again and then a third time. Finally, cursing herself, she quickly rinsed out her mouth then picked up the receiver. "Hello."

"Randi, are you okay? I just talked to Oscar Benjamin, and he told me what happened last night," Eric said.

She closed her eyes and placed her palm against her forehead. "Hell, the police can't even keep a secret here."

"He thought I already knew."

Randi paced across the small room. "No, and if you tell Mom, I'll make you regret it for the rest of your life."

"I think you need to come home."

She stopped pacing and stared out the sliding-glass door toward the water. "To Mom and Dad's? Are you crazy?"

"Then stay at my place."

"Eric, your place is about the size of my car's trunk."

"I don't want you to stay alone, okay?"

She glanced at the bathroom door, behind which she heard the sound of running water. "That seems to be going around."

"Did Zac tell you the same thing?"

"How… Oh, guess you heard from Will or Karl."

"Yes, and I told Will he was a jackass."

She wouldn't have been more surprised if she'd awakened to find her room filled with purple bunnies. "You did? And you're still able to talk this morning?"

"Carol was there and she backed me up."

"I think you and Carol should have married."

"Bite your tongue. And quit getting off topic."

"Listen, I'm not going anywhere. I've already moved hotels once. I'm not going to play musical chairs for this guy."

"Randi, he gutted a dog just to scare the crap out of you." Eric sounded about as close to yelling as she had ever heard him.

"I'm well aware of that. Now get off my case." Her irritation came through loud and abundantly clear. "I'm not stupid, and I'm not going to do stupid things. Not that some of my brothers believe that, but I thought I could count on you."

"You can, you know that. Hell, I told Will he's a jackass and to leave Zac alone. If the police say he was innocent and he passes your test, that's good enough for me."

Randi was stunned into momentary silence. "I...I appreciate that."

"I liked the guy when we worked together. That charge never sat well with me despite the evidence, but I was in the minority and too dumb to take a stand against everyone else. And you can tell Zac I said so."

"He might think hell has frozen over."

After she refused three more attempts to get her to stay with their parents, Eric made her promise to stay safe and to call him if she needed anything. Reluctantly, he said goodbye and ended the call.

"Who was that?"

Randi nearly drooled at the sight of Zac wearing only his jeans and still sporting wet hair from the shower. "Uh, Eric."

"Something wrong?"

Other than she wanted to forget work and drag Zac into bed, everything was peachy. "No. He just heard about what happened last night."

"He's not coming over to beat me up, is he?" Zac asked, then shot her a crooked grin.

Bless Zac for trying to lighten the mood. Did he know she was falling for him a little more every time he did something kind?

"No, you and your jaw are safe for now. Actually, he wanted me to tell you something."

"Oh yeah?" Zac sounded as though he wasn't sure he wanted to hear the message.

"He said he was sorry."

"For what?"

"That he didn't stand up for you when you were charged. He believed you but he was overruled."

Zac stared at her as if she were speaking Portuguese then seemed to realize he was standing there gaping. He rubbed the towel he held over his short, wet hair. "He seemed like the friendliest of the lot."

"He is. He was always the one I was closest to. We thought about things the same way. Well, except today."

Zac tossed the towel back into the bathroom. "What did you disagree on?"

"He wants me to run and hide at Mom and Dad's."

Zac crossed his arms and leaned one shoulder against the wall. Mercy, she really was going to drool.

"Sounds like a good idea to me," he said.

"Don't you start, too. I can't think of a more uncomfortable situation. I'd rather sleep in the Beach Bum."

"Don't tempt me. I might chain you to me so you'd have to stay there at night."

Randi gave him a "just try it" look. "This isn't the first time I've gotten threats. Arsonists don't particularly fancy me."

"Have any of them threatened to gut your dog before?"

Randi shuddered. "No."

"Well, then, this is different. I know I don't have a right to tell you what to do, but if you don't get some backup, I'm sticking by you. Adam and Suz will just have to run the bar until this is over."

Randi stood and stalked to the dresser, rummaged through the piles of clothing. "After what I told you, you ought to know I don't like being treated like a defenseless girl."

Zac moved closer to her. "That's not how I see you."

"Couldn't prove it by me." Where was her other shirt?

Zac grabbed her and pulled her against him. "This is how I see you." He kissed her with such passion her head and heart spun in dizzying circles. His fresh-from-the-shower scent and his smooth, hard chest beneath her palms sent desire surging through her.

After several seconds bordering on brutal, the kiss softened and his hands snaked into her hair, pressing her closer. When he pulled away, it was only far enough that he could speak against her lips. "I see you as a woman I'd give just about anything to spend the day in bed with."

"Oh," she said, more breathlessly than she intended, and she took another step on the road to falling hopelessly in love with the sexy, wonderful, sometimes exasperating man holding her in his arms.

"I know you're strong and smart, but no one is invincible. So you're stuck with me, whether you like it or not."

Zac Parker was a man of his word. For the next two days, he stuck by her like glue, like her shadow, like a few more bad clichés she couldn't think of because his nearness was driving her crazy. Not only was she distracted by how much more she wanted him every day, but he took bodyguarding to the extreme. Attempting to control a control freak tended to irritate her. She could be the poster child for irritation.

By the evening of the second day, she'd had it. When he insisted on checking her room before she could enter, she blew up. "For pity's sake, will you quit! Go home, Zac. Go to the bar. Go somewhere besides two inches from me."

"We've talked about this."

"Yeah, but what I've said hasn't gotten through that bullheaded brain of yours. You're driving me bananas!"

He ignored her as he had the past forty-eight hours. Fine, she'd ignore him. She headed for the shower to get some semblance of privacy.

He *was* driving her crazy. On top of his bodyguard shtick, there'd been no other sexual overtures. Mainly because her sour temper grew with every hour he dogged her steps. Hard to feel romantic when you're ticked off. And to compound her frustration, she'd wake in the middle of the night to find him still sleeping in the chair because of her foul mood, which made her feel ungrateful and bitchy. As she watched him sleep, her body yearned for his even if he was overdoing the guarding detail. If she had to spend another night with Zac in the room, she was either going to go totally mad or cave and drag him into bed. Her libido liked that idea, but her stubborn Cooke pride chastised her for her weakness.

It was almost enough to make her consider Eric's suggestion, but then having four brothers tailing her every move wasn't exactly an improvement.

After she'd taken as long as possible in the bathroom, she opened the door and walked into the main part of the room to find her mother sitting on the end of the bed.

"Mom, what are you doing here?" From the look on her mother's face, it wasn't hard to guess.

"I've come to bring you home. I've already packed your things for you, and Josh took them down to the car. He'll ride with you back to the house."

Randi's temper flared as she scanned the room. No Zac. "That sneaky bastard told you."

"He's concerned." Inga looked into her eyes with

hurt showing in her own. "I can't believe you didn't come to us."

"I'm not exactly everyone's favorite relative."

"You're our daughter. We want to protect you."

"I don't need protecting. I told Zac that a million times. Where'd the snake go, anyway?"

Inga looked confused. "To his bar. He said you told him to leave several times, so he took the opportunity when we showed up. Said you two needed a break from each other."

"Yeah, like, forever."

Inga stood. "Come on, dear. We'll check you out of the hotel then get home before dark."

"The bogeyman isn't coming out just because the sun sets."

Inga grabbed Randi's arm and shook it. "You are coming with me, you hear?" Tears pooled in her mother's eyes. "You're my only daughter, and I can't stand the idea of something happening to you. There's been too much pain in this family. Pain I've done nothing to alleviate," she said, her words full of sadness and shame.

Randi stood staring at the woman who looked like her mother and talked like her mother but who certainly wasn't behaving like the calm, serene Inga Cooke she'd known her entire life.

"If I'm in danger, I don't want to endanger all of you," Randi said, meaning every word but hoping it would make her mom back off, too.

"There are way more of us than there are of him." Inga wiped away her tears. "Please, Randi. Please come back to the house. I'm going to be a nervous wreck if you don't."

All her fight and refusal left her. She followed her

mother to the elevator—anything to take the tortured look out of her mother's eyes.

COULD AN OTHERWISE healthy, twenty-nine-year-old woman have cardiac arrest simply by being anxious? That crazy question ran through Randi's head as she followed Josh and her mother into her parents' house. How had she let her mother talk her into this?

Josh disappeared down the hall with her bags. Randi froze in the foyer, half forgetting how to breathe.

"Come on, hon," her mother said and motioned for Randi to follow her. "We can catch up while I finish dinner."

Now that Randi was inside her childhood home, her mother acted as if she were simply there for a normal visit—before-the-fire normal.

Randi would rather go hide in her room and work, but instead she followed her mom. Maybe if she gave herself a few minutes to adjust to the idea of being here, she'd stop feeling as if a rhino were sitting on her chest. A scary thought occurred to her.

"Mom, does Dad know I'm going to be here?" she asked as they entered the kitchen. The words still hung in the air when Randi noticed her father sitting at the kitchen table working a crossword puzzle.

"Yes," he said.

Randi swallowed past the dryness in her throat. "Hi, Dad."

He nodded.

Just as her mom was about to pull a casserole from the oven, the phone rang. "Oh, that's your aunt Olivia. I forgot she was going to call tonight. Randi, can you get the casserole and pop some rolls in?"

Before Randi could form an answer, Inga left the room to take the call in her bedroom. Randi inhaled deeply and headed for the oven, trying to ignore the tension in the room. She and her father hadn't been alone together since before the accident.

One moment she wished he'd say something, anything. The next she hoped he'd remain quiet. She was afraid of what he might say, that she might fall apart as if she were a little girl again. He didn't speak. All she heard was his breathing and the scratching of his pencil against the crossword page, and Josh going out the front door.

Randi managed to nearly drop the casserole and burn her fingers on the pan when she pulled it from the oven.

"It's good you're here," her father said, making her jump at his sudden words. Had he just said what she thought? Did she dare hope? "Your mother was worried."

Her *mother* was worried.

What about him? she wanted to ask. Was he worried, too? Or had the disability she'd caused pushed her so far from his concerns that he'd rather she stayed at the hotel?

Inga rushed back into the room. "Sorry that took so long. Olivia is a chatty one."

Her mother's forced chipperness combined with her father's distance was too much for Randi. "Everything's out of the oven. I think I'm just going to go to bed. I'm really tired."

Before her mother could object, Randi fled the room without looking at her father. Once inside her old bedroom, she didn't even turn on the light. Instead, she curled up on the bed and let the tears come.

Chapter Ten

Randi went to police headquarters the next morning to check in with Oscar about the threats against her and whether he'd heard anything about the arson case.

"Sorry, Randi. We've got zip," he said.

When she left, Josh strode out by her side. He traded babysitting shifts with Karl when they reached her car. "You all don't have to stick to me like I'm flypaper," she snapped. Maybe she could have Thor use them for chew toys for a bit just to make her feel better.

"You know how Mom is when she gets like this," Karl said.

She did indeed. Inga Cooke was a soothing, calm soul the vast majority of the time, but when she made up her mind to do something, the entire U.S. Army wasn't going to stop her.

And while it was frustrating, it was also nice to feel that maybe her family cared about her again. Will, however, had so far not been part of her guard detail. Avoiding her, no doubt, after their fight at the beach. While it was probably best for them to steer clear of each other, that her oldest brother might be lost to her forever still broke her heart.

Resigned to having human watchdogs, in addition to Thor, she headed for the fire station. At least there, her brothers would wander off and talk to the other guys while she talked to Jack.

"Look what the cat dragged in," Jack said when he saw her come through the door.

She scowled at him.

"Having that good a day, huh?"

"You try going about your business with a shadow a foot taller than you following behind."

"Yeah, heard Inga put the boys to work." Jack frowned as he sat down, and she wondered if his aging joints were bothering him more than he'd ever admit.

Randi sank into the duct-taped leather chair in the office. "What am I overlooking, Jack? It's like the guy can watch my every move, but I can't find evidence to peg who it is."

"The clever ones are the hardest to catch. Not everyone's the stereotypical dumb criminal."

"Well, I wish he'd slip up before I lose my mind." Or more. She damn well wasn't going to lose Thor or her own life. "I was wondering, do you have any unsolved fires in the past couple of years? Even small ones."

Jack sat back in his much-used desk chair.

A memory of her father sitting in that same captain's chair stole her concentration for a few seconds.

"We've had the odd brushfire here and there, trash cans outside businesses, I think one house fire that didn't consume the structure, just torched a deck and the adjoining den."

"Doesn't sound like you have a serial arsonist on the loose."

Jack's gaze narrowed as it always did when an aspect of a case drew his undivided attention. "What made you think we did?"

"Just a guess, which you know I hate."

"Yeah."

Randi sighed and leaned back against the soft leather. "When I finally find this guy, I'm so going to make him pay."

"Any leads on the note and photo?"

"Not yet." She waited for Jack to give her some reassurance, but the words didn't come. Maybe her long string of successes was coming to an end, and he didn't want to point that out.

The phone rang. Randi closed her eyes and drifted as Jack talked to the caller. She hadn't slept well the night before. Being in her old bedroom, knowing her father was only two doors down the hall, had been torture. He talked to her, sure, but in a detached way, as he would to a mere acquaintance rather than his daughter. She'd said she was sorry long ago, but things were evidently never going to be the way they were before the fire.

Not to mention she'd been all hot for Zac, and instead of satisfying that hunger he'd told her family she was in danger so they could help guard her every move. Correction—not *help*. There would be no more guarding of her by Zac Parker. If she saw him, she'd be sorely tempted to run him over for pushing her into this uncomfortable position.

"Okay, I'll see you about seven tonight," Jack said, then hung up the phone.

"Hot date?"

Jack snorted. "Hardly. Unless you count having dinner with the fire chief in Panama City hot."

"He in town?"

"Nah. I'm doing a class over there in the morning."

"You're still teaching those? Seriously, when are you going to retire?"

"When I keel over."

If she thought about it, Jack's refusal to retire made sense. He was divorced, and besides being a firefighter, his only other interest was fishing.

She yawned as she stood. "Well, have a good trip. If you happen along anyone who confesses to the Horizon Vista fire along the way, give me a call."

He chuckled. "I'll do that."

Karl left in the middle of a conversation with one of the firemen to follow her to her car. She had to find the arsonist and arrest his ass before her brothers' constant presence drove her over the edge.

RANDI AVOIDED the discomfort of dinner with her parents by eating some takeout. When she did go home, she forced herself to endure a few minutes of meaningless small talk before escaping to her room. But once inside the familiar space, all she could do was stare at the walls, the furniture and the curtains. Her mother had redone the room in cool mint and white, but it still had the feel of her childhood. Even without the boom box, pinups of teen heartthrobs who didn't have careers anymore and scattered textbooks, her room still held her memories. How she wished she could go back and change things so the close, warm, loving family that had once lived in this house was whole again.

She lay back on the bed and stared at the ceiling, focusing on work so she wouldn't have to miss people under the same roof.

Her eyes were closed when her cell phone rang. She answered, half hoping it was Zac, half hoping it wasn't. "Hello."

"Hey, Randi."

She sat up at the sound of Steve's voice. If he was calling this late, he didn't want to chat about the weather. "What is it?"

"We've had another fire, a hotel in Destin."

"How bad?"

"Total." She didn't like the deep sigh he heaved.

"What?"

"Someone died in this one—a firefighter."

RANDI HADN'T ARGUED when Steve insisted she take backup, though she would have much rather taken someone other than Will. But since Karl was off visiting his soon-to-be in-laws, and Josh and Eric were working, Will it was. It'd taken ten minutes to track him down on his cell. He arrived in sweaty, ratty clothes, silent and surly. What had he been doing? Where had he been?

Once they were in the car and Thor was settled in the back, Randi took a deep breath and broke the silence. "What were you doing when I called?"

"Some work." He looked out the passenger-side window.

"Mr. Verbose as always, I see."

He turned, his eyes narrowed. "Why do you want to know?"

"I'm an investigator. I'm nosy."

"I've noticed."

Will remained silent for a long time. The tension increased like rising water threatening to cut off Randi's oxygen.

Probably ten miles later, he startled her by actually speaking. "I'm building a house on the beach, out on Palm."

Randi glanced at him. "A house?"

"Yes, a house. It's a surprise for Carol, so don't blab."

Her hands tightened on the steering wheel. Damn him, he still made her feel five years old sometimes.

By the time they arrived at the fire scene forty-five minutes later, she couldn't wait to get out of the car. Will seemed equally thrilled by the together time. The acrid smell of smoke still filled the air and her nose twitched. She flashed her credentials and headed for the group of firefighters that looked like command central. When she reached them, they greeted Will first. Normally, this would have annoyed her, but she wasn't about to pick on firefighters who'd just lost one of their own.

"What have you found out?" she asked.

A middle-aged man with the tired appearance of someone who hadn't slept in a week looked at her. "It started on the darkest corner of the building, close to the beach a little after nine. It's been dry, so all the landscaping vegetation caught. Looks like that might've been what set the building ablaze so quickly."

Randi imagined one dried bush catching the next one on fire, then the next and the next until there was a ring of fire around the building.

"Do you know if there had been any opposition to this hotel?"

"You mean like that condo fire over in Horizon Beach?"

She nodded.

"No. This place has been here for ten years or more."

That's what she was afraid of. She thanked the

fireman and guided Thor toward the burned-out shell of a building.

She glanced toward Will. "Keep an eye open for anyone who looks suspicious, anyone who looks a little too interested in what's going on or in me."

"You think it's the same guy? Doesn't seem to have any connection."

"Unless he just enjoys setting fires."

"A serial arsonist?"

"I have to consider it, especially since I'm not coming up with anything else." When they reached the back of the building, she let Thor go but kept close to him. That cruel bastard out there somewhere wasn't getting anywhere near her dog.

"Would you be looking at Parker more if you weren't involved with him?" He didn't try to hide his contempt.

Randi stopped and glared at her brother. "No. As I've said before, there's only circumstantial evidence against him, and that's pretty thin. If you want to get this to stick because you're dying to be vindicated for your state-ments when he was charged or you don't like what he said about our family, you need to let that go."

Will's curse told her she might have hit a bit too close to the truth. Will hated being wrong, always had.

"And I'm not involved with him."

Will snorted. "Could have fooled me."

"You're such a pain in the ass sometimes. I don't know how Carol stands you."

"I just call it like I see it, and I saw you all—"

Randi spun and pushed Will hard in the chest. "Shut up or you'll be walking home. Yes, Zac's a rat fink, but you butted in where you didn't belong. I'm an adult now. Remember that."

To her amazement, Will remained silent as she turned back to her work and started taking notes. She stayed close to Thor as he sniffed the edges of the burned-out area. When they got to a particularly charred corner, Thor stopped and yipped. Randi stirred the ash before Thor stepped on a hidden ember and burned his paws. When she deemed it safe, he took a few steps forward and began to bark. Point of ignition.

RANDI SPENT the next two days working the case in Destin, one brother always at her side. After a while, she got used to them there and even began to have real conversations with them. It helped lift her heart a little, a heart that was missing Zac, much to her dismay. On the afternoon of day two, Jack dropped by the scene of the fire after he finished his training seminar.

"Saw the story about this in the paper," he said when he found Randi doing one more survey before the cleanup crews came in with dozers and dump trucks. "People would pick the driest summer we've had in a decade to start burning everything up."

"I think it's the same guy," she said.

Jack looked surprised but interested. "Back to that again? Lab reports the same?"

"Both gasoline, both lit on the beach side of the building. That alone isn't much. But to have two large fires this close together in time and area is suspicious. And no clear suspects have presented themselves here, either."

"What's the motive? Not the same type of building, and there shouldn't be any controversy around this one. It's been here longer than half the hotels on this street. Hell, we even had an arson investigation training session here a few years ago."

"I think he's getting a kick out of it. Thinks he's smarter than everyone else."

Jack scanned the hotel's shell. "So far he has been."

True. But she was going to nail this guy if she had to interview and do background checks on everyone in Florida.

When she and Karl returned to their parents' house, her father was gone and her mom was just hanging up the phone. "Oh, there you are, dear. That was Zac. He wanted to talk to you."

"Well, he can keep waiting." The unreturned messages on her cell's voice mail should have been a clue that she didn't want to talk to him.

Karl, looking really uncomfortable by the turn of the conversation, grabbed one of the oatmeal-chocolate-chip cookies from the plate on the table and took off.

"Randi, honey, I thought you liked Zac," her mother said.

"Until he decided to call you to haul me home like I was three years old." She took a bite of warm cookie.

"Call me? Zac didn't call me. Eric did."

Randi stopped chewing and stared at her mother. "Eric?" she said around a mouthful of cookie before swallowing. "He's the one who told you?"

"He was concerned. We all were when we heard what that awful person had done to you."

Randi stalked out the door and to her car. When Thor tried to follow, she told him to stay. She had floors to wax with her brothers' butts, and she could do that just fine on her own.

She made it to the fire station just after Karl. Fate was finally smiling on her because all four brothers stared at her as she approached them. But she fixed her gaze

on Eric, the one who was supposed to be on her side.
"You! Of this whole miserable lot, you're the one who
told Mom about the threats? I thought I knew you better
than that."

"Listen—"

"No, you listen." She scanned the line of Cooke
men. D.J., the one fireman on duty not related to her,
suddenly had something to do outside. "All of you. I
know you still think of me as your baby sister, and
even if you don't like me much anymore you still
seem to feel responsible. Well, I hereby release you
of any responsibility. If I get myself killed, it's my
own fault, okay?"

As one, the shocked looks appeared on their faces.
But Eric's was the worst. "Not like you? Why the hell
do you think I told Mom? You're the only sister I've got,
and I'm not going to stand by and let some wacko hurt
you just because you might get your feelings bruised."

She heard his words, wanted to believe them, but she
couldn't let her anger go. "I know I messed up with
Dad." She banged her fist against her heart. "It kills me
to know my mistake put him in that chair. I think about
it every day and wonder why it wasn't me instead. But
I've got to live my life, and that includes doing my job.
You all can't prevent me from making other mistakes
just because you're standing next to me."

Eric took her shoulders in a firm grip. "It's not
mistakes we're worried about. It's you, damn it!"

She scanned her brothers' faces and saw concern
there, for her, not for any huge errors she might make
that would hurt others. Even Will. It finally soaked in.
They still cared about her.

Caught off guard, Randi didn't know how to react,

what to say. Tears welled in her eyes. She turned and walked across the truck bay to hide them. She'd grown up around so many men, it was almost as difficult for her to share feelings as it was for them. But they had.

"I appreciate the concern," she said. She knew the situation called for more, that she might be missing an opportunity for true reconciliation, but she was so full of whirling emotion she was afraid to speak, afraid she'd dissolve in tears and remind them she was a woman, weaker somehow. She was already half-afraid they'd keep up the bodyguard detail after she wrapped up the case and returned to Pensacola.

Her eyes roamed over the fire engine in front of her. Yes, her brothers could be overprotective, but it was because they cared. Maybe the same thing applied to Zac. She turned to leave.

"Where are you going?" Eric asked.

"I have someone I need to talk to." As she walked to her car, she heard footsteps behind her, but she didn't turn to see whose they were. It didn't really matter. She couldn't stop them from following. But if Zac forgave her for making the wrong assumption, her brothers wouldn't want to hang around for long.

ZAC TOSSED his laundry into the dryer with more force than necessary. He should really forget Randi Cooke. Hadn't he learned his lessen the last time he'd dealt with the Cooke family? They were your friend one moment but turned their backs the next. He liked to think it was her family's influence that kept her from returning his calls, but doubt whispered that making the decision to avoid him was all hers. Maybe she didn't think him as innocent as she professed.

But damned if he didn't want her more than any woman he'd ever met. And not just in his bed. Adam would have a field day if Zac ever admitted that simply sitting on the beach with Randi had been the highlight of his past week. She was frustrated by his following her everywhere to ensure her safety, but hell, what did she expect? What kind of guy would he be if he saw that picture of the dog and then let her go on her merry way?

He guessed it wasn't his self-imposed duty anymore. But he sure did miss the way the sea breeze lifted her hair and she swatted at the errant strands like she would a fly. And the brightness of her smile whenever she allowed herself to stop thinking about work long enough to enjoy the parts of life free of criminals and threats. She was like no woman he'd ever met, and that was exactly why he liked her.

That and the blue halter dress.

Just as he pushed the dryer's power button, someone rang his doorbell. He decided to ignore it, not in the mood for solicitors, whether they were hawking products or religion. But it rang a second time, then a third. Okay, either it was important or the world's most persistent peddler.

He didn't expect to see Randi on his doorstep. For a moment, he considered letting her stand there while he refused to answer the door—see how she liked it. But that sounded like something a high school girl would do, so he opened the door and leaned casually in the doorway. She'd made the effort to come see him, hadn't she? "You rang?"

"I'm sorry."

He hadn't been expecting a swift apology, either. "For?"

"Not calling you back. I made an assumption, and I just found out I was wrong."

He crossed his arms. "An assumption, huh? I thought you were Miss Facts Only."

"I am…well, about work I am. Listen, I thought you were the one who told my mother about the photo and the threats when it was actually Eric." She glanced over her shoulder at the street.

There sat Will and Eric in a car parked behind Randi's, not looking their way but with the windows down so they could hear the conversation.

Randi turned her back to them again. "But you can see how easy that assumption was considering I came out of the bathroom to find you gone and my mother sitting on the end of my bed with my bags already packed."

"Next time, ask." He shifted away from the door frame.

Randi put out her hand as if she thought he was about to slam the door in her face. "Please give me another chance."

The pleading in her eyes made him want to wrap her in his arms and soothe away everything negative that dared come near her.

"I'm sorry I didn't ask first before jumping to conclusions," she said. "I ought to know better."

He watched her for a suspended moment, knowing how hard it must have been for her to come to him and admit her mistake. His gut was telling him to give her that second chance, and unlike her, he trusted his gut. He glanced at the brother bodyguards. "You want to come in?" He opened the door farther as tension seemed to drain away from her shoulders.

When Randi passed by, brushing him, his body reacted the way it had the night he'd kissed her on the beach.

"Will isn't going to storm in, is he?"

Her eyes narrowed as she glanced out the door. "No. We've come to a tentative understanding."

He swung the door closed and moved toward her until she bumped up against the back of the couch. "Where's the pooch?"

"With Mom."

"Good," he said as his mouth made contact with hers.

The heat between them shot up as he pulled her closer and deepened the kiss. All the hot, desperate yearning she'd made him feel that night on the beach came roaring back, and this time he wasn't letting anything or anyone get in the way. He lifted his head enough to look into her eyes. "You planning to go anywhere?"

"No."

"Good." He kissed her again, thoroughly so she knew exactly what he was thinking. Then he stepped away, leaving her a little glassy-eyed.

"Where are you going?"

"To get rid of the two-legged watchdogs." He pulled open the front door and walked to the edge of the porch. "You all can go do whatever you do on Friday nights."

Eric, in the driver's seat, turned to talk to Will.

"Trust me, you don't want to stay," Zac said. And with what he hoped was a grin wicked enough to drive Randi's brothers crazy, Zac walked back inside and locked the door behind him.

Chapter Eleven

All of Randi's nerve endings sprang to attention like soldiers at boot camp. When Zac turned toward her, having dismissed her brothers, there was no mistaking the look on his face. He aimed to get her into bed, quickly. And that was okay by her. The sudden need for this man was so powerful it nearly swamped her. The way he walked toward her reminded her of Indiana Jones, James Bond and a lion all rolled into one. Sexy and exciting and dangerous. She nearly growled in response.

Zac took the last steps and wrapped her in his arms, crushing his hard body and hot mouth to hers.

Zac pulled away to take a breath. "Tell me you're positive, because I'm going to have you naked in about three seconds."

She wanted to scream yes! but responded only with, "Positive. Though I don't think I'll be able to look my brothers in the eyes after this."

"Then look at their knees." He captured her mouth again.

And if there was one thing Zac knew how to use well, it was his mouth. Coaxing, tugging, suckling, caressing—it all made her want to collapse in an old-fashioned swoon. It made her lose her mind so much that when she came up for air, she realized he'd maneuvered her into his bedroom. Zac was a man of his word, ridding her of her clothing in about three seconds. She tugged at his like they were on fire and about to consume him.

For a moment, she felt self-conscious being naked with him considering her brothers might still be outside, but the feel of skin on heated skin quickly dissolved her hesitance.

When they fell into the bed, Zac settled a gentle kiss on her mouth and whispered, "Don't think."

She didn't. She lay back with her eyes closed and enjoyed the wet, hungry feel of his lips on her neck, shoulders, breasts. Every delicious sensation he sent rippling through her body made her feel she was going to float up off the bed. By the time he joined with her, it was so easy, so…so right.

Randi gasped and panted and clung to Zac's sweaty back as they poured all their pent-up emotions and need into their lovemaking. When they both found their release, she still clung to him, afraid he and what they'd shared would disappear if she let go. How could she love this man so much so quickly?

But it had to be love. What else could fill her so completely with happiness and fear at the same time? Fear that if she uttered the words, she would lose him before he discovered he could love her, too. She didn't kid herself that sex and love were the same thing to men.

He stirred beside her and nuzzled the side of her neck. "I think I've found another of your talents."

She smiled wide toward the ceiling.

"Are you blushing?"

"Maybe."

Zac laughed as he ran his fingers over her stomach. "Who knew I could embarrass the tough-as-nails Randi Cooke?"

"I'm not so tough." She didn't know why she said it, why she divulged she was more vulnerable than she liked to admit.

Zac lifted to one elbow and looked down into her eyes. "You're tougher than you realize, and the sexiest woman I've ever seen walk down the beach toward my bar."

"Now that last part I doubt. I've seen the women and their itsy-bitsy bikinis strutting by."

"Are they the ones in my bed right now?"

He had a point there.

Zac lowered his mouth to hers and placed a kiss on her lips that was so soft, so tender it brought tears to her eyes. She quickly batted them back, not ready to reveal she'd totally lost her heart to him. She wanted to hold that knowledge close, examine it, delight in it, pray that when this case was over he'd still be a part of her life. How could she go back to the way things were when she knew how it felt to be held like this?

The outside world intruded in the form of the shrill ringing of her cell phone. She glanced over to where it lay in the middle of the pile of clothing, still clipped to the waistband of her pants. She sighed. "I have to answer that."

Zac moved from the bed and got the phone for her, allowing her a full view of his naked body.

He saw her appreciation when he turned around and gave her a wicked wink before planting another heat-stoking kiss on her mouth. He walked into the adjoining bathroom as the phone continued to ring.

Even after he shut the door, it took her a moment to answer the call. "Randi Cooke."

"Did you have to come in from the sea to get to your phone?" Steve asked, sounding harried. Not a good sign.

"Sorry." She wasn't about to explain.

"We've got to get this case wrapped up. The governor's office is breathing down my neck. Seems Oldham is a buddy of his."

"I don't like being pushed, Steve. You know that. Especially when the evidence isn't presenting itself."

"Well, I've got more info for you. We've had an anonymous tip come in. Someone saying he was a guest at the hotel next door claims he saw a Zac Parker running away from the Horizon Vista complex a few minutes before the fire. This Parker was charged in a previous arson case."

Randi's heart, which had been happily bumping around in her chest until now, nearly stopped. That couldn't be right. Zac couldn't have her snowed that completely. She dismissed the accusation. "He was cleared before. And there's no hard evidence indicating he had anything to do with the Horizon Vista fire."

"You want evidence, here's your evidence. Make it stick and wrap it up. We've got other fires to deal with."

The governor must be really pressuring Steve because he normally let her take her time and do the job right.

"That's not reliable evidence, an anonymous tip we have no way of validating."

"You got anything better?" Steve's snippy tone told her how frazzled he was.

The bathroom doorknob rattled. "I'll look into it." She hung up as Zac emerged and slid back into bed with her.

He took her in his arms and held her. It felt so incredibly good, the solidness and strength of him wrapped around her, the strong sound of his heartbeat beneath her ear.

How could she even consider he was an arsonist who had killed one of his own? He wasn't. She believed him, believed in him. She had to because if she was wrong this time, there would be no putting her heart back together.

As SHE DROVE back toward her parents' house later, she thought about the anonymous tip. The tipster had to be mistaken or was the real arsonist. But she wasn't about to tell Steve that and get herself pulled from the case for conflict of interest. The tip showed desperation and increased the pressure to find the real arsonist, and fast. Because he wasn't just an arsonist anymore. Now he was a killer who happened to set fires.

She thought of the story she'd read about the fallen firefighter in the Destin paper—a father with three young children. Randi had been an adult when she'd almost lost her own father. She couldn't imagine what it was like for those little kids. This bastard was going to pay.

Randi was glad to see only her parents' vehicle in the driveway. No battalion of brothers to pass through. After waving goodbye to Zac, who'd insisted on following her home, she edged quietly in through the side door. She hoped she could sneak through the house to her room, but no such luck.

She found her mother standing by the front window watching Zac turn around in the driveway and head off to work.

"I'm sorry about the misunderstanding," Inga said. "I didn't know you thought Zac told me about the threats."

"It's okay. I shouldn't have jumped to conclusions. That's not something I do anymore. Usually."

"Well, I'm glad you and Zac worked it out." Inga smiled and turned from the window.

"Why?"

"Because it's obvious you care for him, dear."

Great. Now not only was she going on instinct rather than facts, but she was transparent, too. If she wasn't careful, she was going to lose her job.

Inga smiled that Mom-knows-all smile and walked over to face Randi. She took Randi's hands in hers. "I'm glad you've found someone who puts a light in your eyes."

She had a light in her eyes? "It may end up being nothing," she said, as if it didn't matter when it mattered a great deal.

"And then, it might be something."

Randi sank onto the arm of the couch. "I've got to solve this case, publicly clear Zac before I can even think about more with him."

"He's still a suspect?" Inga asked, surprised.

"We got an anonymous tip that casts more suspicion on him."

"What do you think?"

"I don't think he did it, but someone out there is trying mighty hard to make it look like he did."

Inga squeezed Randi's hands. "You'll find a way to solve this, and be with Zac. If you find someone you love, you grab him and hold on. Nothing is certain in this life. You take happiness when it comes."

Randi thought of how she'd almost cost her mother the person she loved most. One of the many walls she'd erected inside herself crumbled as if weakened by a blaze. "I'm sorry."

"For what, dear?"

"For what happened to Dad." Her voice caught, as if the guilt and sorrow had become a physical barrier in her throat. She had to clear it to continue. "I'm sorry he came in after me, that he nearly died because of my mistake."

Pain and loss filled Inga's eyes before she lifted her hand to Randi's cheek. "Oh, honey, I'm so glad you were there. If you hadn't fought so hard to get your father out, he would have died. And I'm so happy your father's still here."

"But it was my fault he got hurt, that he was in danger at all."

Inga shook her head. "Listen to me." She paused, took a deep, fortifying breath before continuing. "I know you see what you did as a mistake, but I don't. You feared for that girl's life, so you endangered your own. Yes, I could have lost you and your father, but if that girl had been in there and died while you watched the fire burn, you wouldn't have been able to live with it. I know you broke the chain of command, disobeyed an order, even put lives at risk, but I can't say you were wrong. To me, you're a hero, and I'm so sorry I've not told you that before." Inga shook her head slowly. "I don't know why it's easier to say nothing, but it is."

"I'm no hero." Randi's throat nearly closed with thick sadness and shame.

"Honey, none of us are perfect. Lord knows I'm not, because I've not done the right thing since the accident.

I let your brothers blame you, let them take out their pain by hurting someone who was already in pain. For that, I'm very, very sorry. I was so focused on your father and the boys never made accusations out loud, at least not in front of me, so it was easier for me to ignore it." Inga paused again. "That was wrong. You're my child as much as them, and I should have made the effort, found the strength to stand up for you."

"But—"

"Don't argue with your mother."

Randi and her mother both jerked and looked toward the end of the hallway where Harold Cooke sat in his wheelchair, looking as powerful as he'd been when a younger, walking man. He stared at Randi, his tight expression making her nervous.

"Randi, it's past time you and I had a talk." He spun his chair to the left and rolled toward the deck.

Stunned by the turn of events, Randi followed her father outside. He didn't stop until he was at the edge of the deck. He sat silently for several moments, his back to her, before indicating the top step next to him. "Come sit."

Randi did as her father commanded, feeling almost like a child again, one on the verge of being scolded.

For several excruciating seconds, he said nothing. Then came a long exhale, years in the making. "I won't lie to you," he said. "After the fire, I was very angry, wished I'd died. It killed me to know I'd be stuck in this chair for the rest of my life."

Randi bit down on her lower lip and batted her eyes to keep from crying. Her heart ached at hearing her father speak the words she'd known all along were inside him, festering.

"I was so angry that I wanted other people to hurt, too. I was not easy on your mother when she was just trying to help me. I refused to talk about anything related to work with your brothers. And…well, I ignored you completely. I'm ashamed of the things I felt and thought back then."

"I understand your blaming me. It was my fault," Randi said past that damned painful lump in her throat.

"I did blame you."

The pain in her heart was too much to bear. Why couldn't she just leave and keep up their unspoken agreement of avoidance? It hurt, but not like the sharp edge of the truth.

"But that was grief and anger talking. It wasn't your fault, Randi, and I'm sorry I haven't said so sooner. I'm a stubborn man, not good at saying what I feel."

"But it was my fault. If I hadn't gone back in, ignored Will's order, you wouldn't have been there when that beam fell. You…" Randi's voice broke, and she couldn't hold back the tears anymore. "I'm so sorry."

Her father took her hand, and for the first time since before the fire, she really felt him there. Of course he'd hugged her and given quick pecks on the cheek when he'd seen her, but she'd never really felt he was there. His body had seemed to take action without his mind or heart participating. With the simple squeeze of her hand, she felt she had her father back, and it made the tears flow more freely.

"The way I figure it, there's enough sorry to go around in this family." He lifted her chin, and she looked at his face through watery eyes already puffy from tears. "And there shouldn't be. Randi, I would have done the same thing if I thought a child was in danger and seconds mattered. Anyone with a heart would have, man or woman."

"But I knew the house was about to go. I should have checked outside for the girl before barging back in." Her voice shook as she fought the forgiveness she'd wanted for so long.

"What if she hadn't been outside? Your mother is right. You couldn't have lived with yourself if there had been a child inside and you'd left her to certain death."

Randi shivered at the horrible image.

"When I think about it now, I'm proud of you. If you thought a child was in that fire, you wouldn't have been the kindhearted daughter I love if you'd ignored it."

"But—"

Her father held up his hand. "No more arguing." He glanced toward the dunes. "I've been thinking a lot since you've been here. I shouldn't have allowed my pain to make this family grow apart when it should've come closer together." He returned his hand to the arm of his chair and his gaze to hers. "What's done is done. And now I'm glad I'm alive. If I'd died, I wouldn't have seen my sons fall in love and get married, wouldn't have gotten to spoil my grandson, wouldn't have seen my daughter become the best fire investigator the state of Florida has ever seen." Harold sighed. "I love you, baby girl. I'm sorry I haven't told you that in a long time. And I'm proud of you."

Randi sat stunned, fearing this was all a cruel dream and she'd wake up to find nothing had changed. Her father watched her, as if trying to figure out a puzzle.

"I..." She couldn't hope, could she? It was too dangerous.

"What?"

"I want to…" Why couldn't she say it?

She didn't have to. Her father knew. She saw it in his eyes. After a moment's hesitation, perhaps in which he might be questioning this reconciliation, he opened his arms to accept her.

Randi nearly jumped from her perch and hugged her father. "I've missed you," she whispered.

He patted her awkwardly on the back, as if he'd forgotten how. "You don't have to miss me anymore." His voice sounded thick, choked with emotion. "I'm sorry it took you being in danger to make me realize how much I've missed you."

When Randi pulled away, she noticed they had an audience. Her mother and all four brothers, Carol and little Carson, even Karl's fiancée, Shellie, all stood in the sliding-glass doorway.

Her father noticed them, too. "It looks like your mother's been reading my mind again." He spun his chair toward the rest of the family. "There has been a lot of hurt inflicted and ugly words in this family in the past few years." He looked directly at Will. "It ends today," her father said in his authoritative tone that brooked no argument.

Will shot her a look, different somehow from the way he'd looked at her before, then disappeared inside. Everyone else shifted in discomfort.

Harold Cooke may have spoken, but it seemed his word was no longer law with his oldest son. He stared at the door through which Will had retreated. "I think the thing I miss most is being able to knock some sense into that thickheaded boy."

Something about the way he said it, maybe a hint of the sense of humor her father used to have, made a nervous smile tug at Randi's lips. And then she saw a few more hesitant, shaky smiles in the crowd of her family.

Only Carol's face was tightened by anger. "Yeah, well I can." She turned toward the door, bent on tearing into Will.

"No," Randi said.

Carol stopped and glanced back toward her.

"I'll talk to him."

"No offense, but he doesn't seem to hear you."

"He will this time." She couldn't be sure of that, but she had to try. She'd seen something other than anger in Will's eyes before he'd walked away, something that hit close to home.

As she expected, he wasn't in the house when she did a quick walk-through. When she stepped out onto the front porch, she turned right and saw Will as he disappeared over the dunes at the end of the street. Just where she tended to head when she needed to be alone and think. Maybe that was the root of her and Will's battle—they were too much alike.

She headed for the beach. This was one time she wouldn't leave him alone with his thoughts.

He said nothing when she reached him at the edge of the water. He stared out across the ocean's surface as though he was looking for answers on the horizon.

It didn't matter anymore who was at fault, who was blaming who, she was going to take the first step. "I'm sorry, Will. I'm sorry I didn't listen and stay out of the fire." The words nearly choked her. Deep down, she still believed she was a good firefighter. She'd not acknowledged that grain of truth in a very long time. Still, wasn't her family more important than her pride? "I'm sorry I caused Dad to get hurt."

He exhaled for so long Randi thought he must be trying to totally empty his lungs. She braced herself for the tirade.

"It's me who should be sorry, and ashamed." The shakiness in his voice made Randi look at him. Tears pooled in his eyes. Will never cried, not even when Grandpa Cooke had died. And he'd been as close to Grandpa Cooke as a grandson could be.

"Will?"

"It was my fault."

"Your fault? How the hell could it be your fault? You weren't even in the fire." It clicked as the last word drained away.

"Exactly," he said. "I should have gone after you. Then Dad wouldn't have been in there."

She stared at him and the familiar look she'd seen on his face earlier now made sense. "All this time, you've blamed yourself inside while on the outside you've been blaming me?" she asked, anger making her voice rise.

He said nothing. Words weren't necessary when the truth was as obvious as the water in front of them.

A new anger rushed up from deep within her. "Why? Why have we gone through this? Did it do either of us a damn bit of good? Because it sure hasn't done Dad or anyone else any favors." She took several steps away so she didn't hit him as she had the last time the two of them had stood on the beach.

"I should have made him stay outside, gone in myself."

Her well of anger flowed over. Randi spun and jabbed her finger at him. "Stop it! I'm sick of the guilt, the anger. We made our choices, and they had dire consequences, but do we have to pay for it the rest of our lives?"

The sight of the tears in Will's eyes spilling over almost undid her, but she kept on.

"We can't go back and undo what happened. Lord knows I've wished that a million times. But I can tell you from experience that guilt is only going to tear you to pieces inside until you don't recognize yourself anymore. It won't do you any good, not Dad, not Carol or Carson. It just eats you alive."

The pain in his eyes deepened. "That's what it's been like for you, too?"

How could a man be so thick he'd not realized that by now? She stared back at him. Maybe it was hard to see when all you did was argue.

"Yes."

Will looked back out across the waves. "Seems my mistakes kept compounding." For the first time she could remember, Will sounded drained, tired to the core. Guilt did that to a person, too.

"Maybe Dad's right. Maybe it's time to leave the past in the past and move on," she said.

Will turned his head slowly to look at her again, an expression of confusion on his face. "You could do that? After what I just told you?"

The importance of the moment weighed on Randi. This was a crossroads if there ever was one. "I can if you can." She wanted to grab on to the lure of a fresh start and go forward instead of looking back all the time.

Will shook his head, and Randi's heart sank. Maybe too much hurt lay between them to mend.

"I was wrong all along," he said. "You were never weak. You're stronger than the rest of us put together." He shook his head again. "I can't believe you didn't punch me before you did."

An unexpected snort escaped her. "Don't think it didn't cross my mind."

For the first time in ages, Will leveled a hint of a smile her direction. But it quickly disappeared. He drew in a shaky breath quite unlike him. "I have no right to ask, but can you at least think about forgiving me? Not for my sake, but for—"

"You're forgiven."

Will stared at her with disbelief. "Just like that?"

Randi blinked against her own tears. "Just like that. I'm tired, Will. I don't want to do this anymore."

Not being the overly demonstrative type, Will didn't crush her in a brotherly bear hug. He just nodded and said, "Thank you."

Honestly, they were probably a long way from putting things fully in the past, but Randi didn't mind. They'd taken the first step, and that was enough for now.

"You're not going to tell the others about…" He gestured toward his face, toward the evidence of his tears.

A long-buried part of her younger self surfaced. She crossed her arms. "How much you going to pay me?"

Will's eyes narrowed. "Pipsqueak."

"Lugnut."

Funny how two childhood nicknames could say more than a million "I'm sorry's."

RANDI COULDN'T BELIEVE how much difference a day could make. It seemed as if her entire family, Thor, even the house itself had let out a collective sigh of relief the previous evening when her father had declared the Cookes' cold war against Randi over.

She looked around her parents' dining room table and watched as her brothers and father took turns examining her case notes, determined to help her find the answers she sought. When she'd told them she didn't believe the arsonist was Zac, they hadn't questioned her—even when she'd told them about the so-called eyewitness.

"Hell, Steve ought to know there are all kinds of flakes who call in tips that have no basis," her dad said.

"Besides, it's fairly obvious that whoever is really behind this wants Zac to take the fall," Eric added.

She shook her head. The change in atmosphere was almost enough to make her believe aliens had swept in from the sea and replaced her family with more friendly, compliant beings.

Karl looked at his watch. "Gotta go."

"What's she got you doing today?" Will asked with a smirk.

Karl walked toward Will, and said, "China patterns, if you must know," and whopped his older brother on the side of the head as the rest of the men snorted with laughter.

Randi laughed, too, and smiled so wide she thought her face might crack. Her family was on the road to recovery. Now, if she could solve this case and figure out what was going on in Zac Parker's brain besides sweaty, mind-melting sex, life would be perfect.

After Karl's departure, the laughter died away and they all dug back into the case notes.

"Damn, I've never seen an arson where the guy didn't leave some clue behind," Josh said.

"Makes you wonder how long he planned this," her father said.

That someone planned this sort of thing—a fire that destroyed, that killed—sent a Minnesota-in-winter shiver down Randi's spine. The depths of hell would freeze over before she let him do it again.

Chapter Twelve

Randi woke with her face pressed against a pile of documents atop the desk in her room. The edge of the file folders had dented a crease into her cheek. Thor was stretched across the bed sawing logs like he was going for the Nobel Prize in Snoring. Not for the first time during this investigation, she wished she and Thor could switch roles. Sure, she'd have to sniff through ash, but now she'd be the one indulging in carefree sleep rather than twisting her brain, trying to squeeze answers out of it.

She stared down at the various case files detailing unsolved arsons she'd had Hannah at her office send her. Then she eyed the Florida map, full of pushpins identifying arson locations. Small towns, cities. Locales in every corner of the state. The only connection she could find was ignition by gasoline. Easy enough to get, available to every age and socioeconomic group.

If the fires were connected, the all-over-the-map nature indicated the person either traveled to set his fires or set fires as he traveled for another reason. She pressed against her forehead with the heel of her hand. What was it? Just looking at the files and map made her head hurt. She decided she needed a long shower before she tackled them again.

The connection clicked while she was lathered to the hilt. She stopped working the shampoo into her hair and stared at the bathroom tiles. Could it be she'd been on the right track early on? Was the reason no clues were left because the person behind the Horizon Vista fire, and perhaps even other unsolved arsons, was indeed a firefighter? Not Zac, but one of his former colleagues.

The thought made her stomach turn. Had she worked alongside a serial arsonist with not even a clue?

She rushed through the rest of her shower, brushed her teeth and quickly dressed while running the names of firefighters through her head. Hopefully, her suspect wasn't someone local. For once, she hoped she was dead wrong.

With renewed energy, she slipped back into the chair and started going through files, checking the names on reports, the list of all the firefighters who'd reported to certain scenes, who'd been the first to arrive. She only looked up when her mother brought her a fresh banana muffin and a glass of orange juice.

Her lists grew as the morning progressed. Desperate to make some sort of link and yet dreading it, she kept working, skipping lunch by telling her parents she wasn't hungry.

Again and again, she went through the files and stared at the names, willing one of them to stand up and scream its guilt. Maybe there was no connection between the fires. The unsolved cases were all over the place as far as type of structures burned, and the fires were started with a common incendiary device.

But maybe that was by design. Wouldn't a firefighter

know the fires wouldn't stand out as connected if he kept them simple? Chills swept over Randi's skin. The property destruction was bad enough, but what about Aaron Jamison, the firefighter who'd lost his life in Destin? What about her father? That fire had been ruled arson, but the culprit never found. What if it was the same arsonist?

She thought back to each of the fires she could remember, trying to recall whether anyone had acted oddly in the aftermath. Nothing. She opened the folder for the Kissimmee auto parts store fire. This one she remembered because she'd seen the building fully engulfed. She and the other four members of her department attending the class in Kissimmee had heard the sirens in the middle of the night and raced to the fire. The blaze had been huge, shooting into the night sky like the fireworks at nearby Disney World.

Something tugged at the back of her mind, but no matter how hard she tried to pin it down and identify it, it kept edging away, playing hard to get.

Feeling achy and sluggish, Randi decided to try a different tactic. Perhaps if she went for a run, she'd jar the answer loose from its hiding place. When she passed through the kitchen, her parents were sitting at the table reading the paper. She had to keep her latest line of thinking from them. Investigating firefighters might not sit well, and she couldn't bear to risk her renewed family ties—not unless she had proof.

"You're going running?" Worry showed on Inga's fair face.

"Yeah, I'm aching from sitting." She bent to kiss her mother on top of her head. "Don't worry. I'm taking Thor and my cell."

It took her a few minutes to get into the rhythm of her run. Without the early-morning coolness and quiet, it proved more difficult to concentrate. She'd gone barely half a mile when she stopped, the elusive bit of information floating to the surface like the flotsam bobbing in the tide.

As Thor realized she'd stopped and turned back toward her, she imagined the faces of the men with whom she'd attended that training session in Kissimmee. Eric, Karl, Harvey Tanner, Mark Stone. The name of the course flashed in her memory as if she were looking at the brochure—Arson Investigation for the Small Fire Department. Randi ran back to the house, Thor beside her. She was still sucking in air when she called the office.

"You solved the case yet?" Hannah asked.

"Hopefully soon."

"Good, because the governor's office called again this morning, and Steve is about to have a stroke."

"Listen, I need you to find some information for me and e-mail it as fast as you can."

"Sure, I don't have anything else to do," Hannah said, her words rich with sarcasm.

"Hannah," Randi pleaded.

"Okay, fine. What do you need?"

"The list of attendees at an arson investigation course taught in Kissimmee four years ago, in July. Look at the list of the unsolved arson files you sent me and see if there were any training courses taught near those fires on the dates they ignited."

"What's going on?" Hannah's tone shifted to concern, as if she knew the direction Randi's mind was traveling.

"Maybe nothing. Let's hope so."

She paced as she waited for the information to arrive in her e-mail in-box. Thor gave her hand a big lick. Thankful for his safety and hopefully the end of the case, she hugged him hard against her, then ruffled the fur on his head.

"What's got you so anxious?"

Randi looked up to see her father sitting in the doorway.

"A hunch. I'll let you know if it pans out."

"Okay. Your mother and I are about to leave. Karl and Eric are going to stop by after they get off work."

Randi nodded then listened as her parents went out the front door, locking the dead bolt behind them.

After thirty minutes, Randi found eleven names in an e-mail from Hannah.

Eleven…eleven fires that coincided with firefighter training courses. Nausea welled up in her stomach. She was glad her parents had left the house to attend the retirement reception of one of her father's friends in Panama City. They wouldn't be back until that night, giving her the room she needed to spread out her work across her desk and bed without worrying who might see the rosters.

She began cross-checking the names, growing frustrated when it seemed the theory might not hold. The most any one firefighter was listed was three times. And five firefighters fell into that category. The odds were firmly against all five being involved with a serial arson plot. Arson was typically a solo act. Plus, some of the fires didn't match up with any of those five. Randi rested her forehead against her palm and stared at the reams of paper in front of her. Why couldn't she figure this out?

A name caught her attention. At the top of the first roster was the instructor's name. Jack Young.

She flipped through the other ten rosters, her heart sinking further with each flip of a page. Jack Young was the instructor or co-instructor in eight of the courses, including the one in Kissimmee. The other three, a student. No. That couldn't be right. A coincidence, that was it. But wasn't she always saying that coincidences were more rare than snow shovels on the Gulf Coast?

She had to be one hundred percent positive before she said anything. Not only was her professional life on the line, so was her renewed relationship with her family, particularly her father, who'd been friends with Jack for more than forty years.

Her father. Jack. Oh God, what if Jack had set the fire that nearly killed her father and her? She shook her head. How could she even consider Jack? He'd always been like a member of the family. He'd eaten more meals at her family's dining room table than some members of her family. When she'd been young, she'd called him Uncle Jack. That's why he'd been so upset by her father's accident. Or was there more there, perhaps guilt? Her skin went clammy at the idea. She prayed she was totally off base. But she had to find out, and before her parents returned home.

She stared at the names for a couple more minutes, hoping some other possibility would present itself. The first unsolved fire on her list occurred about ten miles from where he was teaching a course in Fort Lauderdale. The newest, the Destin hotel, was on his way between Horizon Beach and Panama City. He'd stopped by to see the aftermath.

The sick feeling in her gut increased. Not only had Jack been like a part of the Cooke family, she'd sat across from him and discussed this case more than once.

Could she have been so blind as to not see the truth sitting in front of her? Or was it possible this was one gigantic coincidence?

So many questions ran through Randi's head, but the main one was "Why?" How could he endanger so many people? Destroy so many lives? Why?

She wasn't going to find the answers sitting in her childhood bedroom. She dialed the station, and with each ring her heartbeat increased. When Jack answered, she nearly yelped. "Hey, Jack."

"Randi, I was just thinking about you, wondering how the investigation is going."

"Slow. This one is kicking my butt, and it's embarrassing."

"Can't win them all, hon."

He'd called her "hon" a thousand times, but this time it made her skin crawl. And he was wrong. She could win them all. She had a perfect record, but this one had nothing to do with her professional life. This was personal.

"Guess not," she said, continuing her charade. "Got a few minutes? I'd like to swing by and run some theories by you."

"Sure. Always have time for you."

Was she imagining his enthusiasm sounded forced? If he was indeed behind the arsons, she couldn't let him guess she had any clue he might be involved. She couldn't give him time to prepare a defense. Best to continue to play dumb and see where it led.

After changing into work clothes, she headed for her car with Thor. She considered leaving him behind, but if she showed up at the station without him, Jack would know something was up. And she wanted to keep him in the dark until she could be sure her hunch was right. Once in the car, she sat and considered calling Steve to fill him in. Even though it was the middle of the day and there would be plenty other people around the fire station, her gut told her to tell someone where she was going. But in case she was wrong, she didn't want to tell anyone in her family. That left Zac. She wasn't exactly sure where they stood now, but this was business, not pleasure.

She punched in the number to the Beach Bum. "Is Zac there?" she asked when Suz answered.

"No, he's supposed to be in later this afternoon."

"Okay. Can you tell him to call Randi when he gets in?"

"Sure thing."

After unsuccessful attempts at reaching him at home and on his cell, Randi called both again and left a brief message about her plans. That done, she sat a couple more minutes, dreading doing her job more than she ever had.

Well, it wasn't going to get any easier just because she was avoiding it. She started the car and headed for the station.

When she arrived, Jack was outside firing up the grill the guys used on a regular basis to barbecue chicken and grill steaks. It wasn't any secret the best place to eat in Horizon Beach was the fire station.

"What's on the menu today?"

Jack looked up and smiled the same smile she'd seen since she was a little girl. "Barbecue ribs. I sent Eric out with a shopping list. Got dinner plans?"

She forced a smile. "I think I do now."

Jack chuckled. "It'll take a few minutes for this to heat up. Come on in. I just made a big jug of lemonade." He turned and headed toward the open doorway in front of the Number 2 engine. The slight limp in his right leg made him look like the grandfather he was.

She followed Jack and was several feet inside the station when she realized no one else was there. Alarm bells clanged in her head. The station was always staffed by at least two firefighters.

"Did you send everyone shopping?"

Jack looked around as if he didn't realize what she was talking about at first. Then he looked toward the trucks. "Oh, no. The rest of the guys are at the Kiddie Kare doing a fire safety program. Little kid came in last week with his daddy's lighter, and the teachers figured it was time for a lesson about how dangerous fire is."

Indeed.

"When are they supposed to be back?"

Jack looked at her with an odd expression, and she hurried to cover her bobble.

"I have to be careful how many people I talk to about this case. The fewer people who know specifics, the more likely I am of finding out who the culprit is."

It felt like a lame answer considering how many times she'd talked to the guys about the fire, but thankfully Jack seemed satisfied with it. She resisted the urge to sigh in relief. Instead, she motioned for Thor to follow her into Jack's office. When they were sitting across from each other, Jack leaned back and asked, "So, what's the latest?"

She spoke as if she knew nothing suspicious about him, hoping she was wrong. And if not, hoping he'd confess. "You know I've been beating my head against the wall, looking at all the people who didn't like Oldham. Anyone who might have wanted to get back at him for everything from his arrogance to the way he obscured the ocean view of some of the residents. Well, now I'm wondering if I was barking up the wrong tree."

"What do you mean?"

"What if this has nothing to do with Oldham at all? What if we've got ourselves someone who likes to play with fire and the high-rise was too tempting to resist?"

Jack leaned forward, listening intently. "You tossed out that theory before, but I assumed nothing came of it since you didn't mention it again."

"It was a last-resort thought. I didn't have evidence pointing to or away from that possibility."

"And now you do?"

"Maybe. I had a hunch this morning, and after doing some more research I've found some interesting patterns."

Jack's face tightened almost imperceptibly. It wasn't the look of a comfortable man, and once again Randi hoped the reason was because he was a firefighter to the core and sickened by the thought of someone setting fires for fun.

"What kind of patterns?"

"Do you remember that auto parts store that burned several years ago while we were at the training session in Kissimmee?"

Something that looked momentarily like panic flickered in Jack's eyes, and Randi's heart sank.

"Yeah, if I remember correctly, the paint cans were flying out of there like bottle rockets."

She swallowed against her dry throat. God, this was going to be awful. "I remembered that fire this morning when I was looking over some files about unsolved arsons across the state. A little more digging revealed that eleven of the unsolved cases coincided with firefighter training sessions." She watched his reactions, but he managed to keep them under control. She strained her ears, hoping one of the guys would return. But she couldn't stop questioning Jack now. He'd know for sure she'd figured it out. And she wasn't giving him the chance to flee.

"You think a firefighter started them?"

"It's a possibility." Her sadness seeped into every word.

"I thought you'd decided Parker was clear in all this."

"It's not Zac's name that I connected to all eleven sessions."

Jack stared back at her, and she saw the moment he knew why she'd come to the station to talk to him. The moment she accepted that her hunch was right. Damn, damn and double damn.

"Why, Jack?" Her question came out strangled as she fought the hurt of betrayal.

"Why what?" Jack affected a look of confusion.

"Why did you set all those fires? You're a firefighter, for God's sake."

Jack's head snapped back as if she'd slapped him. "What the hell are you talking about?"

"Your name is the only one that's connected to every training session." Her tone begged him to prove her wrong.

"You know I taught those all over the state. I've been doing that for damn near twenty years."

"And all that travel gave you the perfect opportunity to torch buildings in new areas far from home, making it more difficult to find a pattern."

Jack's face reddened. "I gave you the benefit of the doubt, even stood up for you with your dad. Now I'm wondering if he was right, that you really aren't cut out for this type of work."

She stared at the man across from her, her insides ripping to shreds and anger rising within her as she considered her next words. "Was it you? Did you set the fire that hurt Dad?" Lord help him if he did because she might leap across the desk and beat him, old man or no.

Jack sank back in his chair and pitched the pen he'd been holding onto the top of his desk. "You need a vacation, a long one, because you're not thinking clearly." He gave her a concerned expression, but she wasn't fooled. It was as if she was seeing him for the first time, and she didn't like what she saw.

"I can't believe how we trusted you."

Jack pointed at her, jabbed his finger like a weapon. "If you don't stop, you're going to force me to call Steve and report that you're making unfounded accusations. You'll lose your job."

"No, Jack, it's you who'll lose your job. And your freedom for what you did. It wasn't just buildings. You destroyed dreams, businesses, lives. A firefighter died!"

Jack gripped the arms of his chair. "Stop it, Randi, before you say something you regret."

"I won't, not until you tell me the truth. I want to hear it from your own mouth." Randi's voice rose with each word, her anger swelling inside her until all the fond memories of Jack were replaced with the terrible knowledge he'd never been the man she'd thought him to be.

"I'll never admit something I didn't do. You're spouting no more than coincidences, circumstantial evidence at the best."

"When the lab finishes going through all the catalogued evidence, my guess is they'll find something…a fingerprint, a hair, something that will prove you set those fires."

"Oh, honey, I hate to see you throw away your career like this. You can't take another mistake on your record." He shook his head slowly, as if saddened to see she'd lost her grip on reality.

Was he delusional? Or playing for time to figure a way out of this horrible mess?

She couldn't stand it anymore. Time to end this. She stood and reached for her cell phone to call the police.

"Put the phone away."

Randi glanced at Jack. Her breath caught in her throat and nearly choked her. The .38 was no bigger than any other, but at the moment the end of the barrel pointed toward her looked like the mouth of a cannon.

Chapter Thirteen

Thor growled next to Randi. She stared at Jack, his weathered, scarred hand wrapped around the gun. This had to be a nightmare.

"I can't let you do this," Jack said. "You don't understand."

Did he actually think there was a rational explanation for arson? For killing and maiming?

Jack gestured with the gun. "Put the phone on the desk."

She thought of arguing, but she didn't know how stable Jack was. And too much was at stake here. She placed the phone on the desk. Part of her wanted Eric to hurry back to the station. Another wanted him to stay far away from this danger.

Oh, God, what about Zac? She remembered his threatening words about the arsonist. He'd put himself in harm's way for her, she knew that. But she couldn't live with herself if she was the cause of someone else she loved getting seriously injured—or worse.

She had to figure a way to get out of this without anyone getting hurt—not her, not Thor, not Zac or her brothers, not even Jack. She wanted him alive so he could answer for what he'd done.

"Push it toward me," Jack said.

She stared at the older man. "You started the fire that caused my father to never walk again."

"Neither of you should have gone back in." His voice lowered, almost as if he'd momentarily forgotten she was there. "No one was ever supposed to get hurt."

"But they did. You killed someone, Jack. How could you? You were supposed to protect people."

"I did protect them. And I didn't kill anyone. People do dumb things and get themselves hurt." Jack shook his head as he gripped the gun harder. "Why didn't you listen? I tried to tell you to stay away." He actually sounded sad, his tone the same as that used by her parents when she'd been a child about to be punished for misbehavior. The whole "this is going to hurt me more than you" speech.

She had to get out of the room before he totally lost it and fired. She didn't think he wanted to shoot her, but she wasn't taking the chance. In his mind, she might have left him no choice. Her cell rang, startling them both. She slowly reached for it.

Jack shoved the gun in her direction. She considered telling him it would look more suspicious if she didn't answer her phone, but then that would indicate she'd told someone where she was going. Instead, they stared at the phone until it stopped ringing. She imagined a message going to voice mail while she sat there with a gun pointed at her chest. The phone rang again.

"You told someone, didn't you?" Jack asked, his face appearing older than before.

"What, that I was coming here?" Please let her acting

skills remain intact. She'd never had a problem before, but this was Jack. He'd known her since the day she was born.

"Oh, Randi, why have you pushed me into this corner?"

"Just give up and let it be over."

"I can't. You don't understand. None of you do."

Hoping to buy time, she said, "Then help me understand." She'd swear she could see him age in front of her.

"Do you know what it's like to have everything taken away from you? To have no power whatsoever to make things the way you want them to be?"

She did, but she didn't speak, hoping that now he'd started, Jack would keep talking.

"My mom, my wife, and now my career—all taken from me." He gripped the gun harder, judging by his white knuckles.

She knew his mom had died when he was young— good Lord, had he started setting fires that long ago? His wife had divorced him when Randi was too young to really know what that meant or why it'd happened.

"What about your career?"

Jack shook his head slowly. "Always second-best to the Cookes."

"How can you say that? You're Dad's best friend." At least until her dad found out the truth.

"And I've always lived in his shadow, always a few steps behind or a few rungs below. I love him like a brother, but I hate him, too."

The betrayal she felt probably showed on her face.

"Did you know your brothers are trying to force me out, to retire? They're trying to take away the last thing I have left."

"You gave up your right to that uniform the first time you set a fire," she said, her voice sharp.

"No one was supposed to get hurt," Jack said, pleading with her to understand. "I just needed something I could control. Fire, that I can control."

"But you didn't control it, did you? My dad is proof of that."

His expression changed, hardened. He didn't have the look of insanity, more that of a trapped animal.

A car braked to a halt outside, followed by doors slamming.

"It's over, Jack. Just put down the gun before you make things worse."

"No." The way he said it spoke of desperation, as did his motion of raising the gun.

Randi didn't think, just acted. She leaped across the desk, trying to dislodge the gun from Jack's hand. Though she was in excellent shape, younger, and had surprise on her side, Jack reacted quickly, throwing up his forearm and catching her under the chin. Her head snapped back, sending pinpricks of light floating before her eyes. She slipped and fell backward onto the floor, cursed as she tasted blood where her teeth cut her lip.

A black blur zipped by her, accompanied by the sound of enraged dog. Thor. Teeth bared, growling.

Jack screamed, Thor yelped. Randi focused on the scene as Jack took aim. "No!" Randi lunged for Jack again. Her vision went scarlet as she slugged Jack in the jaw.

He reacted with a fist to her stomach that left her shocked and gasping. Even after everything, it was hard to believe he'd hit her. And for a nearly seventy-year-old man, he still packed a stunning punch. Her head swam, but she forced herself to stay upright. She was going to make him pay. She winced as she righted herself in time to see Jack pulling back his fist to hit her again.

He never got the chance. The door slammed open, bouncing off the wall, and a stream of men ran into the room. She was still trying to catch her breath when she saw Zac, his face contorted with rage, grab Jack and throw him against the wall. Her brothers followed, each wanting a piece of the man, collectively looking like a pack of wolves descending on a kill.

The room turned to chaos as Jack fought back. Office supplies went flying and chairs were knocked over. Thor continued to bark and growl. And then everything froze when a shot blasted, echoing off the walls. Zac staggered backward. When he spun around, blood was pouring from his forehead.

Randi's heart froze in terror. "Oh, God, no!" She rushed forward as Zac started to go down. She caught one of his arms while Eric caught the other. Will growled like Thor. He and the rest of her brothers tackled Jack, but their struggle faded behind Randi as she directed all of her attention to Zac. Blood from his forehead was running down into his hair. It stood out in stark contrast to the uncharacteristic paleness of his face.

Almost as soon as she knelt beside him, several police officers and paramedics rushed through the door. One of the paramedics urged her away from Zac's side so he could attend Zac's wound.

"There's so much blood," she said. The world spun around her, and another paramedic guided her to a chair. She tried to push him away, but Eric held down her hands as the paramedic checked her over, cleaned and bandaged a cut on her cheek. Throughout it all, she didn't take her eyes away from Zac, afraid he'd die and leave her if she did.

Why had she put herself in this position of getting hurt again?

"I'm okay," she heard Zac say as he tried to lift himself up. But from the look on his face, the action caused his head to swim.

"Lie back," one of the paramedics said. "It looks like just a flesh wound, but we're going to get you checked out to be sure."

The sound of handcuffs clicking together drew Randi's attention. She watched as the police cuffed Jack and read him his rights. Jack caught her gaze.

"Randi, don't let them do this to me. It's all a misunderstanding."

She said nothing but sent him a stare so full of hatred she wouldn't be surprised if it burned him. That hatred fueled her right now because part of her had died inside when she'd realized her assumption about his guilt was correct.

As the paramedics moved Zac onto a stretcher, she broke eye contact with Jack, tuning out his pleas and not caring if she ever saw him again.

There wasn't room for her in the ambulance, and Eric refused to let her drive. As she watched the back of the ambulance in front of them while they headed to the hospital, guilt began to eat at her.

"I shouldn't have called him," she said half to herself.

"It's a damn good thing you did, or things might have turned out a whole lot worse."

"Worse? Zac got shot!"

"And you heard the paramedic. It's only a nasty flesh wound. They're just taking precautions."

Randi directed her gaze out the passenger-side window but didn't really see the familiar scenery as it passed by.

"You could have been killed," Eric said.

She knew he was right, even though it made her heart want to cleave in two to admit it. Tears leaked out of her eyes and ran down her cheeks. "This is going to hurt Dad so much."

Eric reached across and squeezed her hand. "Don't worry about that now. And don't you dare blame yourself. This wasn't your fault."

She knew that, but she couldn't help feeling she was always hurting the people around her.

Once they arrived at the hospital, Randi rushed up to Zac's side as he was unloaded from the ambulance. When he saw her, he reached for her hand.

"Are you all right?"

She offered him a shaky smile. "Better than you at the moment. You should really learn to duck."

"I'll remember that next time."

She hated letting go of his hand, but she had to as the paramedics wheeled him inside. Eric guided her not to a waiting room but toward one of the curtained E.R. examination areas. She balked. "I'm fine."

"Then this won't take long."

Randi started to argue some more, but she noticed Will, Josh and Karl stepping up behind Eric. She had no doubt they would carry her kicking and screaming into the examining room if she didn't go of her own accord. Without a word, she turned and allowed a doctor and nurse to examine her injuries and test her for a concussion.

When she was declared to be perfectly healthy, if bruised and shaken, she strode out past her waiting brothers. "Told you I was fine." She tried to walk farther back into the E.R., where they'd taken Zac, but a nurse redirected her to a waiting area. She couldn't sit still so ended up pacing the hallway, blaming herself for Zac's injury. Her brothers displayed some good sense and left her alone.

"You're waiting for Zac Parker?" a doctor asked her as she turned to head down the corridor again.

Her heart started pumping harder. "Yes, is he okay?"

"He's fine. He's going to have a doozy of a headache for a while, but he's very lucky. The bullet just hit skin, barely missed the bone. He'll be ready to leave in a couple of minutes."

A lump grew in her throat. Barely missed the bone. God, because of her he could have had a hole blown in his skull. "Thank you," she whispered past the painful lump.

The doctor nodded then headed back down the hall to deal with other patients. Randi glanced over to where her brothers were watching her. She didn't say anything as she turned and walked out of the hospital.

She ended up at the beach. For the longest time, she sat in the sand and watched the waves go in and out. Their movement mirrored the feelings roiling inside her. She wanted desperately to be with Zac, but she almost felt like the Angel of Death sometimes. Because of her actions, no matter how good the intentions, two people had almost died. First her father, now Zac.

No matter how hard she tried she couldn't get the horrible image of Zac spinning around with blood streaming down his face out of her head. A mere fraction of an inch could have cost him his life. A sob broke free, and all the emotion she'd been holding in since she'd confirmed Jack's guilt came pouring out. She dropped her head to her arms crossed over her upturned knees and let all the fear and pain and betrayal escape.

She had no idea how long she cried, but by the time her final tears dried, her eyes were puffy and itchy. And she ached to see Zac, to kiss him and tell him how sorry she was for everything. She lifted her battered body from the sand, knowing that her external injuries would heal long before her emotional pain. But she wasn't going to think about Jack now. She ignored everyone she passed as she left the beach and started weaving her way along Horizon Beach's streets toward Zac's house.

She had no idea what would happen between them in the future, what would happen with any aspect of her life in the next few days, but for now she only wanted one thing. To be with Zac.

When he opened his front door in response to her knock, the first thing she saw was the bandage on his forehead and how his complexion looked paler than normal. She fought a new wave of tears.

"I'm so sorry," she said as she wrapped her arms around him.

"Shh. You don't have anything to be sorry for."

She pulled back from him and ran her fingertips gently over the bandage. "I almost got you killed."

He wrapped her hand in his. "This was Jack's fault, not yours." He pulled her inside and closed the front door. He led her into the kitchen and poured her a glass of water. "Where did you go?"

She shook her head as she took the glass. "I had to get away, to think for a while."

"You should have gone to your parents' house to get some rest. You need to take it easy for a few days."

"What I need is you." Need and yearning burned in her blue eyes, but he couldn't move. Instead, she set the glass of water aside and walked slowly toward him. "But I don't want to hurt your head."

"You're not going to hurt me," he said, his voice husky with rising desire.

She touched her soft lips to his neck. He groaned in response. Then her tongue made contact with his skin. The resulting surge through his body made him pull her close and attack her mouth with his. Within moments, they shucked what little clothing they wore and stood naked in his kitchen, grasping, groping, touching, kissing, stroking. In the whirl of motion, Randi ended up seated on the corner of his kitchen table, and he stood between her legs, gasping for breath.

When she grabbed his face and kissed him like she was trying to suck out his soul, he resisted no longer and joined her atop the table. He vibrated with need, with desire, with a feeling so intense he thought surely he would ignite and burn away to nothing. Randi held him so tightly and rose to meet him over and over with so much intensity. He lost track of time, of everything but the woman in his arms. Her breathing came faster and more ragged, her body went rigid. Her eyes closed as she reached…reached…reached…then collapsed beneath him.

Her completion undid him and with little more movement he achieved his own release. It took him several seconds to realize they now lay sprawled across his kitchen table, naked and sweaty and sated, and that two of his four chairs had been overturned. He hadn't even noticed when that happened. He'd never, ever had such fantastic sex, the kind to which a man could easily get addicted.

Zac raised up on one arm and looked down at Randi. Her long hair had come loose from its customary band and lay fanned out around her. Damn, she was beautiful. And for some reason she'd chosen to be with him—at least for now. Nothing could make him prouder, happier or feel more fully like a man. He loved her so much it was frightening.

"Are you okay?" he asked.

She nodded. "I wanted to feel alive, to feel something good."

"Glad to oblige." He ignored the pinch in his chest.

Randi lifted her hand to his cheek. "But I wasn't using you. No one else would have made me feel the way you do. You're an amazing man, Zac Parker."

He rubbed his thumb across her lips, bent to kiss her cut gently. "You're pretty amazing yourself, Miranda Cooke."

She took a deep breath. "I was so scared when I heard that gun go off, when I saw all the blood pouring down your face."

He kissed her forehead. "I'm fine. The least little head wound bleeds like crazy." He ran his fingertips gently along the side of her cheek. "I can't tell you how scared I was when we were trying to get to the station. I would have never forgiven myself if I hadn't gotten there in time." He lay down and pulled her close against him, assuring himself she was indeed whole and safe.

"We're all fine now, except…"

Zac heard the pain of her unspoken words. "I'm sorry it was Jack."

She closed her eyes. "I've never felt so betrayed."

"I know. But he'll never be able to do it again."

"How do you not look at everyone and wonder if they're not as they seem after something like this?"

He let the question hang in the air for a few seconds. "I don't know, but my gut tells me this type of thing doesn't happen too often. Don't start second-guessing yourself. You're a good investigator. All you have to do is look at your record to know that. One difficult case isn't going to change all those successes."

Randi turned in his arms. "You're so good for me."

Zac's heart felt oddly full. "Nice to know I'm good at something besides pouring drinks."

Randi smiled a saucy smile then climbed atop him. "I can think of something else you're excellent at."

"That so?"

She licked her lips. "Just how strong is this table?"

Chapter Fourteen

Randi drifted on a hazy cloud between sleep and waking, vaguely aware she and Zac were still sprawled on the kitchen table. She'd blush at the image they must make if it hadn't been so fantastic and exactly what she'd needed. She opened her eyes to see daylight had nearly faded and Zac watching her.

"Hello." She should be embarrassed, but she wasn't. That told her all she needed to know about her feelings for Zac. She didn't doubt she loved him, but guys were an odd breed. Did he feel that depth of emotion for her? Something about the way he acted around her told her he did, but she wasn't going to rush anything despite the day's events making her yearn to grab everything she wanted and pull it to her. Well, actually, she'd already done that with Zac—twice. She smiled.

"That looks like the smile of a contented woman."

"Just thinking how glad I am that I'm here instead of my parents' house."

"Yes, I imagine they would frown on having their dining room table used in such a way. As it is, I may never be able to eat at this table again."

She smiled again, hoping he never forgot their lovemaking. Goodness knows she wouldn't. On the heels of staring death in the face, she'd never felt more alive than when in his arms, clinging to him as he made love to her. Yes, it was technically just hot, ravenous sex, but it still felt like love to her. Intense, bone-deep love.

A loud knock on the front door made them both jump.

"Randi!"

"Oh crap, it's Will." Randi scooted off the table and searched for her discarded shirt.

Zac followed and slipped into his jeans. Then he grabbed Randi and kissed her deep and hard. "I'll take care of it."

She kissed him back, thanked him, then hurried toward the bedroom.

Zac couldn't help smiling as he watched her run down the hall.

The banging came again. "Open the door, Parker."

Despite Will's command, he seemed startled when Zac pulled the door open. Zac hadn't even bothered to put on a shirt or shoes or fix his mussed hair. The house probably smelled like sex anyway.

"Is Randi here?" Will asked.

"Yes."

"Is she okay?"

Zac propped his palm against the edge of the door. "Yes."

"I want to see her."

"Why?"

Will scanned the room behind Zac. "To make sure she's okay."

"You don't trust me?"

"Today, I don't trust anyone."

Zac knew the feeling. "She's resting."

"It's okay, Zac," Randi said from behind him.

He glanced back. She still wore the well-loved ex-pression on her face. He couldn't stop smiling at her. She hadn't tried to hide what had gone on between them, and he loved her even more because of it.

"Will, I'm fine, really."

A vein pulsed in Will's neck. Zac imagined big brother wanted to rip him to shreds for touching his little sister. But Randi wasn't little anymore. She was a grown woman, a fantastic one at that, and the Cooke boys had to get used to it.

"You're sure?" The genuine worry in Will's question told Zac the broken relationship between Randi and her oldest brother was on the mend.

"Positive. I'll be back later." She looked at Zac, and her eyes spoke more than words. "Maybe in the morning."

Will didn't like this answer, but he couldn't pull Randi kicking and screaming from the house. "Call if you need anything."

"Okay."

Will didn't budge. Randi disappeared down the hall-way again.

Will turned his gaze to Zac. "I'm going to trust you. But if you hurt her, I'll make you wish you were dead."

Zac stared Will right in the eye. "If anything hurts her, I already will be."

FORCING HERSELF to leave Zac's arms the next morning was harder than she'd ever imagined. Even without the words, she'd never felt so loved, so protected, so impor-tant to a person. But she needed to check on how her family was taking the news about Jack and call Steve.

And maybe some hours away from Zac would reveal what she should do next. Maybe the new day would disclose whether the intensity of feelings on both their parts was real or a reaction to the scare of the day before.

She wished she could avoid the questions and knowing looks she knew awaited her, but dealing with the fallout of the case and Jack's betrayal trumped her discomfort. The two-mile walk through the early morning actually helped her feel better despite what she knew had to happen in the days ahead. When she slipped into the house, her mother nearly knocked her down with a hug.

"Oh, thank God you're home. I worried about you all night."

"I'm sorry you worried. I just…needed to be with Zac. I…" Her voice broke. "I almost lost him."

"I know, sweetheart." Inga hugged Randi harder and rubbed her hand over her daughter's hair like she had when Randi was a little girl. After a few moments, she pulled back.

"You love him, don't you?" Inga looked calmer now, a mother's worries allayed.

What would be the purpose of denying it? Sure, she didn't know where they were headed, if anywhere, but denying the feeling served no purpose. Inga already knew anyway.

"Yes."

Inga smiled and nodded. "Good, because that man loves you more than any I've ever seen. Will said an army couldn't have gotten past Zac yesterday, and only a foolish man would have tried."

"Will said that?"

"Yes." Her mom took a few steps and sank onto the

end of the couch as if her legs wouldn't hold her up anymore. Tears sprang into her eyes. "God, I still can't believe it was Jack. When Eric called to tell us, I thought it was a cruel joke."

"I'm so sorry."

Inga squeezed Randi's hand. "I'm just glad it's over, that you're not in danger anymore."

Randi glanced past her mom. "How's Dad?"

"Devastated, though very glad you're okay. He left a few minutes ago. He just needs some time alone to come to terms with this."

Randi stepped back, her heart breaking for all her father had lost.

After a few more minutes of talking to her mom, Randi headed to the shower, hoping the hot water would ease her aches. Despite the events of the past twenty-four hours, part of her heart felt strangely lighter. It felt so good to have her family back, to have this case solved no matter how painful the conclusion, and to know Zac Parker was willing to be her knight in shining armor if she learned how to let him.

"YOU'VE GOT IT bad, haven't you?" Adam sat in his customary spot at the bar, giving Zac his "another single guy bites the dust" look. "You haven't seen Randi in a couple of days, and you look like you're about to frown yourself into a face cramp."

"I've got work to do. So does she."

"Horizon Beach isn't that big. You both can do your work and still manage to bump into each other."

Zac didn't need Adam reminding him that Randi was possibly avoiding him. They'd talked on the phone and all her explanations sounded genuine, but doubt still twinged in his gut. He tossed down the towel, frustrated that he was analyzing a relationship far more than any good, red-blooded American male should.

"Hey, don't let it get you down," Adam said. "Try as we might to avoid it, sometimes the big *L* word catches us anyway."

"How would you know?"

"Just because I'm free now doesn't mean I always have been. It's not necessarily a bad thing," Adam said, a hint of a past story in the way he said it. He took a long drink of his beer.

Zac looked at his friend and saw something he'd never seen before—seriousness that wasn't laced with teasing. But after a few awkward moments, it disappeared, leaving the consummate bachelor behind.

Adam glanced at the beach then slid off his bar stool. "I think I'll throw a line in the water and see what comes up."

Zac looked toward the beach and saw Randi a few feet away.

"Hey, Adam," she said as they passed.

"Randi. Are you ready to leave this bum and run away with me yet?"

She smiled at the joke. But when she turned toward Zac, instinct told him she was indeed leaving.

"How are you?"

"Better, considering. Sorry I haven't come by. I've been spending some time with my family and helping wrap up the investigation here."

"No need to explain." He wiped down the bar, trying to appear laid-back.

She placed her hand atop his. "You see, Zac, that's the thing. I've never felt the need to explain to anyone before."

He held her gaze. What should he say?

She looked away first and pulled her hand back. "I'm headed back to Pensacola. The crap is hitting the fan about this case."

"I've seen the news. You going to be okay?"

She nodded but looked sad at the same time. "Yeah. I mean, it's still hard getting my mind around it all, but the reality is starting to sink in."

"How's your family?"

"Hurt, angry, but glad I'm okay. We're mending fences."

"That's good." She stared at him again, as if she expected him to say more. What was he supposed to say? Blurt out that he loved her, that he didn't want her to go? Would it matter if he said those words? Or would he just be left standing here like an idiot when she walked away back to her life, her job?

What the hell! "Randi, I—"

Randi spoke at the same time, drowning out his words. "I'll call you when I get home, okay?"

He swallowed the declaration and nodded. This didn't feel right anyway. He had absolutely no experience at this type of thing, but there should be a right place and time for telling a woman you loved her. This wasn't it. He'd messed up things with her once before and was afraid of doing so again.

Her smile wavered. "Okay, I guess I'll talk to you soon."

"Yeah, soon." Why couldn't he say something more important? He pointed at a stool. "There'll always be a seat open for you, even if I have to kick Adam off his."

With another shaky smile, she turned and walked out of the bar. He wanted to run after her, but he just stood there watching her trudge through the sand toward the parking lot, hoping he wasn't watching her walk away for the last time.

RANDI WAS TIRED of guessing the extent of Zac's feelings for her. He cared, that much was obvious from their phone conversations over the past three weeks while she wrapped up the Horizon Vista case and tied up other loose ends. He'd even sent her a bouquet of bright, mixed flowers that morning for her birthday. Her mother had helped him pick out all her favorite flowers.

She still couldn't believe her parents had gone to the Beach Bum and her father had apologized to Zac. Randi was happy that he was back on speaking terms with her family, but knowing they were all down in Horizon Beach talking about her was disconcerting, to say the least.

She pulled into the parking lot nearest the Beach Bum, got out and inhaled deeply of the ocean breeze. Yes, this was right. She loved it here, and chances were very good the man she loved was only a short stroll away. She wasn't one to take big leaps of faith, particularly where her feelings were involved, but special circumstances called for special measures.

She smoothed her white eyelet tank and sky-blue capris then descended the wooden steps from the parking lot to the beach, Thor by her side. As she walked through the sand, the lively activity at the Beach Bum drawing her like a lighthouse beacon, she hoped her appearance would stun Zac into voicing his true feelings. She'd lived with enough men growing up that she knew they weren't always the most intuitive creatures. Sometimes you had to figuratively bang them upside the head to get them to realize they needed to *say* things instead of assuming people just *knew* them.

She smiled when she saw Adam in his customary spot, being his charming self next to a leggy redhead in a hot-pink minidress.

Randi stood at the edge of the bar watching Zac fill drink orders. It felt so good to see him. She didn't know if it was the time apart or whether the fact that she loved him had sunk in more, but he looked a million times better to her than when she'd left. And he'd looked damned near irresistible then.

Adam spotted her and paused in his conversation to say something to Zac, who immediately turned toward her. She smiled, and when he smiled back she nearly squealed with joy. She stepped up into the bar then headed for the empty stool on the nearest end of the bar. He'd said there'd always be a seat open for her, and he was right.

She slid onto the stool just as Zac moved in front of her. "What'll you have, ma'am?"

"I'll take a glass of your best lemonade."

He smiled and prepared her drink. When he slid it in front of her, their hands touched and held. "I didn't know you were coming down this weekend."

"Kind of a spur-of-the-moment decision."

"Happy birthday," he said. "I'm glad you liked the flowers."

"They're beautiful. They're actually in my car," she said as she gestured toward the parking lot. She took a long drink, gathering her courage to surge forward. When she set the glass back down, she said, "Actually, my birthday is why I'm here. I couldn't think of a better place to spend it than the beach, and there's something down here I want for my birthday."

"What's that?"

She looked him directly in the eyes. "You."

The only way she knew he'd actually comprehended her words was the slight smile and the tightening of his grip on her hand.

"I'll be glad to oblige."

Okay, it was now or never. "And not just for tonight."

He smiled a quite self-satisfied, devilish smile. "How long were you thinking?"

Randi felt she must be going up in flames, and Zac was smiling as he fanned them. Must…think…straight.

"A long time, perhaps…forever."

Zac's teasing smile fell away. Randi's stomach knotted as she tried not to think she'd mistaken his feelings. She couldn't have misread all their conversations, the way he'd held her, comforted her, made love to her like he'd die if he didn't.

"What about your job?"

"I quit," she said. "And I've got five days of freedom before I start my new job as Horizon Beach's newest firefighter. Whatever will I do with the time?" She had to inject some teasing into the conversation or she was going to crack with wanting.

Zac stared at her for several seconds. "Why?"

"Lots of reasons. I'm tired of traveling all over the state, not having a life outside work. I miss my family, the beach and…you. I'm taking a chance here, but I have a feeling it's the right one." She paused. "I love you, Zac. I've never loved anyone more, and it's a little scary."

Again, Zac stared at her for interminable seconds. Or was it minutes? Had she been as wrong about him as she had about Jack?

"I know what you mean," he said.

"What?"

"That it's scary." He looked so intense, but then a light filled his eyes and spread across his face. All of a sudden, he looked as if he'd never been happier. "I love you, Miranda Cooke."

Miranda. Her name sounded beautiful and full of love coming from him. She smiled wide, her heart dancing in her chest.

"Oh, for the love of Pete, kiss the woman already!" Adam said, followed by cheers from the rest of the bar's patrons.

Randi looked around to see everyone watching them.

"I think I will," Zac said.

Randi turned in time to see Zac round the bar, pull her off the stool and into his arms, and kiss her with such passion she was quite sure this was her best birthday ever. Over the rush of blood in her ears, she heard the wild clapping, whistling and cheering of the bar's customers. And the distinct barking of Thor from just outside.

Zac pulled away enough to spot Thor.

Randi looked at her sidekick as well. "I think we have the black Lab seal of approval."

Zac looked back at her and smiled. "Well, I certainly want to keep your dog happy."

And then he kissed her again. This time, all the cheering and barking faded away. There was just Zac, and that was quite all right with her.

* * * * *

Turn the page for a sneak preview of
AFTERSHOCK, *a new anthology*
featuring New York Times *bestselling author*
Sharon Sala.

Available October 2008.

n⬤cturne™

Dramatic and sensual tales of paranormal romance.

Chapter 1

Nicole Masters was sitting cross-legged on her sofa while a cold autumn rain peppered the windows of her fourth-floor apartment. She was poking at the ice cream in her bowl and trying not to be in a mood.

Six weeks ago, a simple trip to her neighborhood pharmacy had turned into a nightmare. She'd walked into the middle of a robbery. She never even saw the man who shot her in the head and left her for dead. She'd survived, but some of her senses had not. She was dealing with short-term memory loss and a tendency to stagger. Even though she'd been told the problems were most likely temporary, she waged a daily battle with depression.

Her parents had been killed in a car wreck when she was twenty-one. And except for a few friends—and most recently her boyfriend, Dominic Tucci, who lived in the apartment right above hers, she was alone. Her doctor kept reminding her that she should be grateful to be alive, and on one level she knew he was right. But he wasn't living in her shoes.

If she'd been anywhere else but at that pharmacy when the robbery happened, she wouldn't have died twice on the way to the hospital. Instead of being grateful that she'd survived, she couldn't stop thinking of what she'd lost.

But that wasn't the end of her troubles. On top of everything else, something strange was happening inside her head. She'd begun to hear odd things: sounds, not voices—at least, she didn't think it was voices. It was more like the distant noise of rapids—a rush of wind and water inside her head that, when it came, blocked out everything around her. It didn't happen often, but when it did, it was frightening, and it was driving her crazy.

The blank moments, which is what she called them, even had a rhythm. First there came that sound, then a cold sweat, then panic with no reason. Part of her feared it was the beginning of an emotional breakdown. And part of her feared it wasn't—that it was going to turn out to be a permanent souvenir of her resurrection.

Frustrated with herself and the situation as it stood, she upped the sound on the TV remote. But instead of *Wheel of Fortune,* an announcer broke in with a special bulletin.

"This just in. Police are on the scene of a kidnapping that occurred only hours ago at The Dakota. Molly Dane, the six-year-old daughter of one of Hollywood's blockbuster stars, Lyla Dane, was taken by force from the family apartment. At this time they have yet to receive a ransom demand. The housekeeper was seriously injured during the abduction, and is, at the present time, in surgery. Police are hoping to be able to talk to her once she regains consciousness. In the meantime, we are going now to a press conference with Lyla Dane."

Horrified, Nicole stilled as the cameras went live to where the actress was speaking before a bank of microphones. The shock and terror in Lyla Dane's voice were physically painful to watch. But even though Nicole kept upping the volume, the sound continued to fade.

Just when she was beginning to think something was wrong with her set, the broadcast suddenly switched from the Dane press conference to what appeared to be footage of the kidnapping, beginning with footage from inside the apartment.

When the front door suddenly flew back against the wall and four men rushed in, Nicole gasped. Horrified, she quickly realized that this must have been caught on a security camera inside the Dane apartment.

As Nicole continued to watch, a small Asian woman, who she guessed was the maid, rushed forward in an effort to keep them out. When one of the men hit her in the face with his gun, Nicole moaned. The violence was too reminiscent of what she'd lived through. Sick to her stomach, she fisted her hands against her belly, wishing it was over, but unable to tear her gaze away.

When the maid dropped to the carpet, the same man followed with a vicious kick to the little woman's midsection that lifted her off the floor.

"Oh, my God," Nicole said. When blood began to pool beneath the maid's head, she started to cry.

As the tape played on, the four men split up in different directions. The camera caught one running down a long marble hallway, then disappearing into a room. Moments later he reappeared, carrying a little girl, who Nicole assumed was Molly Dane. The child was wearing a pair of red pants and a white turtleneck sweater, and her hair was partially blocking her abductor's face as he carried her down the hall. She was kicking and screaming in his arms, and when he slapped her, it elicited an agonized scream that brought the other three running. Nicole watched in horror as one of them ran up and put his hand over Molly's face. Seconds later, she went limp.

One moment they were in the foyer, then they were gone.

Nicole jumped to her feet, then staggered drunkenly. The bowl of ice cream she'd absentmindedly placed in her lap shattered at her feet, splattering glass and melting ice cream everywhere.

The picture on the screen abruptly switched from the kidnapping to what Nicole assumed was a rerun of Lyla Dane's plea for her daughter's safe return, but she was numb.

Before she could think what to do next, the door-bell rang. Startled by the unexpected sound, she shakily swiped at the tears and took a step forward. She didn't feel the glass shards piercing her feet until she took the second step. At that point, sharp pains shot through her foot. She gasped, then looked down in confusion. Her legs looked as if she'd been running through mud, and she was standing in broken glass and ice cream, while a thin ribbon of blood seeped out from beneath her toes.

"Oh, no," Nicole mumbled, then stifled a second moan of pain.

The doorbell rang again. She shivered, then clutched her head in confusion.

"Just a minute!" she yelled, then tried to sidestep the rest of the debris as she hobbled to the door.

When she looked through the peephole in the door, she didn't know whether to be relieved or regretful.

It was Dominic, and as usual, she was a mess.

Nicole smiled a little self-consciously as she opened the door to let him in. "I just don't know what's happening to me. I think I'm losing my mind."

"Hey, don't talk about my woman like that."

Nicole rode the surge of delight his words brought. "So I'm still your woman?"

Dominic lowered his head.

Their lips met.

The kiss proceeded.

Slowly.

Thoroughly.

* * * * *

Be sure to look for the AFTERSHOCK *anthology next month, as well as other exciting paranormal stories from Silhouette Nocturne.*
Available in October wherever books are sold.

nocturne™

NEW YORK TIMES BESTSELLING AUTHOR
SHARON SALA

JANIS REAMES HUDSON
DEBRA COWAN

AFTERSHOCK

Three women are brought to the brink of death...
only to discover the aftershock of their trauma has
left them with unexpected and unwelcome gifts of
paranormal powers. Now each woman must learn to
accept her newfound abilities while fighting for life,
love and second chances....

Available October wherever books are sold.

www.eHarlequin.com
www.paranormalromanceblog.wordpress.com

SN61796

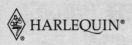

HARLEQUIN®

American ★ Romance®

HOLLY JACOBS
Once Upon
a Thanksgiving

AMERICAN DADS

Single mom Samantha Williams has work,
four kids and is even volunteering for the
school's Thanksgiving pageant. Her full life
gets busier when Harry Remington takes
over as interim principal. Will he say
goodbye at the end of his term in
December…or can Samantha give
him the best reason to stay?

*Available October 2008
wherever books are sold.*

LOVE, HOME & HAPPINESS

www.eHarlequin.com

HAR75236

REQUEST YOUR FREE BOOKS!
2 FREE NOVELS PLUS 2
FREE GIFTS!

Heart, Home & Happiness!

YES! Please send me 2 FREE Harlequin American Romance® novels and my 2 FREE gifts (gifts are worth about $10). After receiving them, if I don't wish to receive any more books, I can return the shipping statement marked "cancel." If I don't cancel, I will receive 4 brand-new novels every month and be billed just $4.24 per book in the U.S. or $4.99 per book in Canada, plus 25¢ shipping and handling per book and applicable taxes, if any*. That's a savings of close to 15% off the cover price! I understand that accepting the 2 free books and gifts places me under no obligation to buy anything. I can always return a shipment and cancel at any time. Even if I never buy another book from Harlequin, the two free books and gifts are mine to keep forever.

154 HDN EEZK 354 HDN EEZV

Name _____ (PLEASE PRINT) _____

Address _____ Apt. # _____

City _____ State/Prov. _____ Zip/Postal Code _____

Signature (if under 18, a parent or guardian must sign) _____

Mail to the **Harlequin Reader Service:**
IN U.S.A.: P.O. Box 1867, Buffalo, NY 14240-1867
IN CANADA: P.O. Box 609, Fort Erie, Ontario L2A 5X3

Not valid to current subscribers of Harlequin American Romance books.

Want to try two free books from another line?
Call 1-800-873-8635 or visit www.morefreebooks.com.

* Terms and prices subject to change without notice. N.Y. residents add applicable sales tax. Canadian residents will be charged applicable provincial taxes and GST. Offer not valid in Quebec. This offer is limited to one order per household. All orders subject to approval. Credit or debit balances in a customer's account(s) may be offset by any other outstanding balance owed by or to the customer. Please allow 4 to 6 weeks for delivery. Offer available while quantities last.

Your Privacy: Harlequin is committed to protecting your privacy. Our Privacy Policy is available online at www.eHarlequin.com or upon request from the Reader Service. From time to time we make our lists of customers available to reputable third parties who may have a product or service of interest to you. If you would prefer we not share your name and address, please check here. ☐

HAR08R

SPECIAL EDITION™

BRAVO FAMILY TIES

Tanner Bravo and Crystal Cerise had it bad
for each other, though they couldn't be more
different. Tanner was the type to settle down;
free-spirited Crystal wouldn't hear of it.
Now that Crystal was pregnant, would
Tanner have his way after all?

Look for

HAVING
TANNER BRAVO'S
BABY

by *USA TODAY* bestselling author
CHRISTINE RIMMER

Available in October wherever books are sold.

Visit Silhouette Books at www.eHarlequin.com   SSE24927

#1 *New York Times* Bestselling Author

DEBBIE MACOMBER

Dear Reader,

I have something to confide in you. I think my husband, Dave, might be having an affair. I found an earring in his pocket, and it's not mine.

You see, he's a pastor. And a good man. I can't believe he's guilty of anything, but why won't he tell me where he's been when he comes home so late?

Reader, I'd love to hear what you think. So come on in and join me for a cup of tea.

Emily Flemming

8 Sandpiper Way

"Those who enjoy good-spirited, gossipy writing will be hooked."
—*Publishers Weekly* on *6 Rainier Drive*

On sale August 26, 2008!

MDM2578

Romantic
SUSPENSE

**Sparked by Danger,
Fueled by Passion.**

USA TODAY bestselling author

Merline Lovelace

Undercover Wife

Secret agent Mike Callahan, code name Hawkeye,
objects when he's paired with sophisticated
Gillian Ridgeway on a dangerous spy mission
to Hong Kong. Gillian has secretly been in love
with him for years, but Hawk is an overprotective
man with a wounded past that threatens to
resurface. Now the two must put their lives—
and hearts—at risk for each other.

Available October wherever books are sold.

Visit Silhouette Books at www.eHarlequin.com   SRS27601

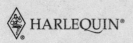

HARLEQUIN®

American ★ Romance®

COMING NEXT MONTH

#1229 HOLDING THE BABY by Margot Early
The State of Parenthood
When Leah Williams agrees to carry a child for her younger sister, Ellen, she isn't prepared when Ellen turns up pregnant! Leah, already a single mom to four-year-old Mary Grace, is left…holding the baby. And to complicate matters further, domineering Mark Logan, the donor father, wants to be a part of their child's life.

#1230 FINALLY A BRIDE by Lisa Childs
The Wedding Party
Running out on her wedding is the only way Molly McClintock can avoid making the biggest mistake of her life. But running to her childhood friend Eric South could land her in even more trouble. The returning war hero is igniting enough sparks to turn friends into lovers for life. Could that walk down the aisle be far behind?

#1231 THE INHERITED TWINS by Cathy Gillen Thacker
Made in Texas
Raising her orphaned niece and nephew and struggling to keep her Texas ranch afloat doesn't leave Claire Olander much time for relationships. Until Heath McPherson comes to Red Sage Ranch. When the gorgeous banker gets his first eyeful of the sexy, spirited single mother, it isn't only the *twins'* future he's thinking about…

#1232 ONCE UPON A THANKSGIVING by Holly Jacobs
American Dads
Between her four kids, her job and volunteering for the school's Thanksgiving pageant, Samantha Williams isn't looking for a new man in her life. But Harry Remington isn't a stranger—the interim principal was her childhood friend. Will he say goodbye at the end of his term in December…or can Samantha give him the best reason of all to stay?

www.eHarlequin.com

HARCNM0908